Mighty Mighty MONSTERS

THE MONSTER CROOKS

STONE ARCH BOOKS
a capstone imprint

Mighty Mighty Monsters are published by
Stone Arch Books, A Capstone Imprint 1710 Roe
Crest Drive, North Mankato, Minnesota 56003
www.capstonepub.com

Library of Congress Cataloging-in-Publication Data
O'Reilly, Sean, 1974–
   The monster crooks / by Sean O'Reilly ;
illustrated by Arcana Studio.
      p. cm. -- (Mighty Mighty Monsters)
   Summary: The Mighty Mighty Monsters help the
police solve an art heist.
   ISBN-13: 978-1-4342-3216-8 (library binding)
   ISBN-10: 1-4342-3216-6 (library binding)
   ISBN-13: 978-1-4342-46103 (paperback)
   1. Graphic novels. [1. Graphic novels. 2. Monsters-
-Fiction. 3. Art thefts--Fiction.] I. Arcana
Studio. II. Title.
   PZ7.7.O74Mn 2011
   741.5'973--dc22

2011003443

Printed in the United States of America
in Stevens Point, Wisconsin.
012014
007959R

THE MONSTER CROOKS

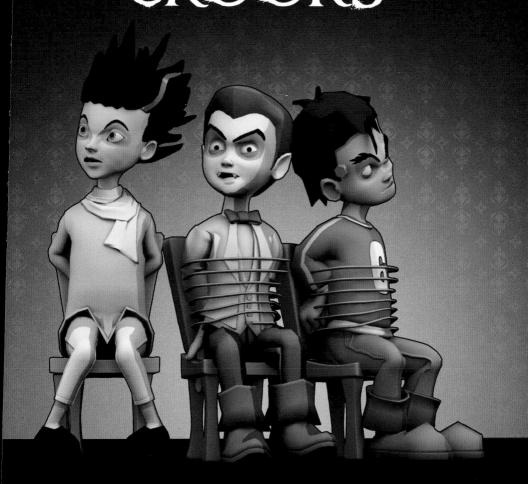

created by
Sean O'Reilly

illustrated by
Arcana Studio

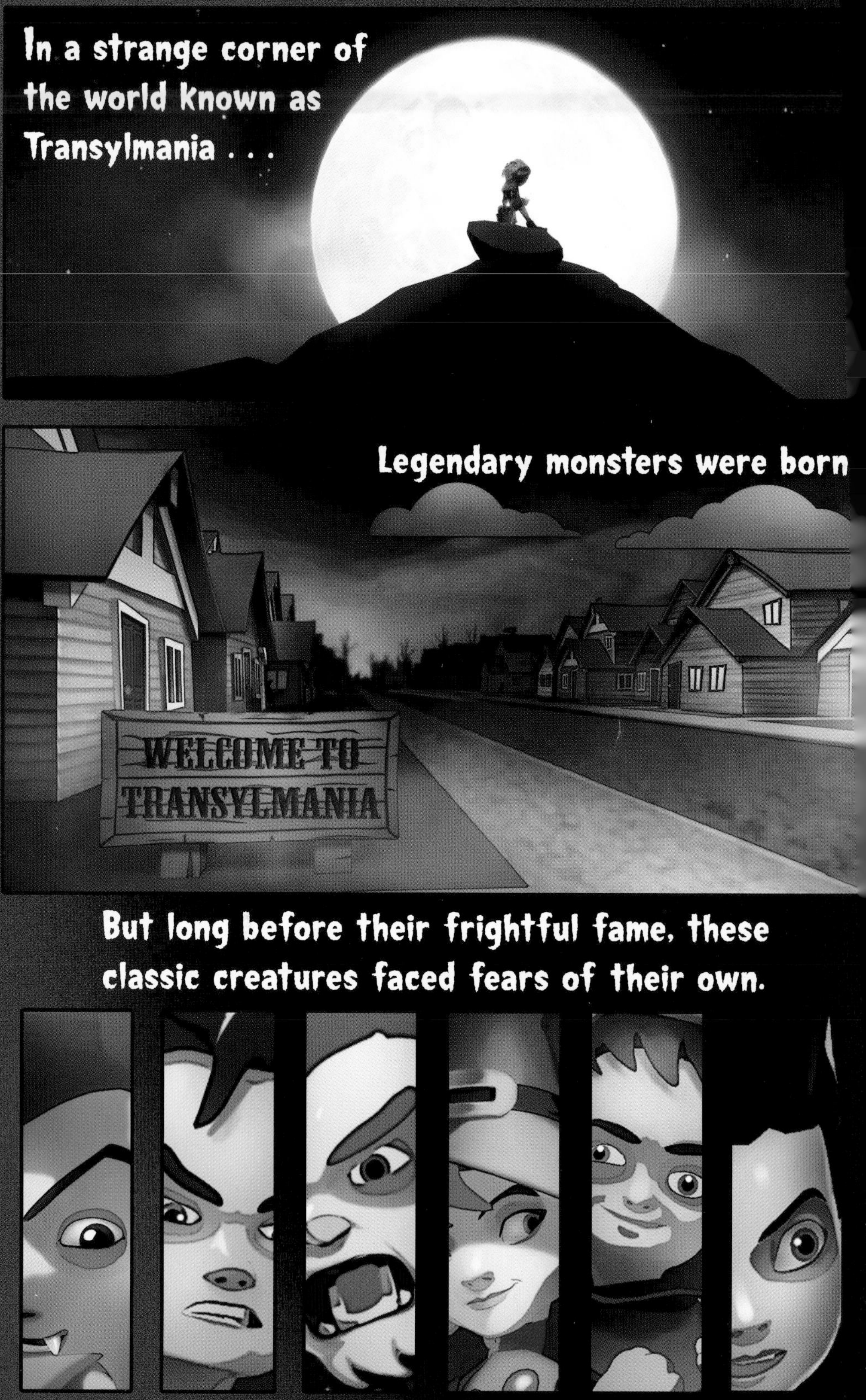
In a strange corner of the world known as Transylmania . . .
Legendary monsters were born
WELCOME TO TRANSYLMANIA
But long before their frightful fame, these classic creatures faced fears of their own.

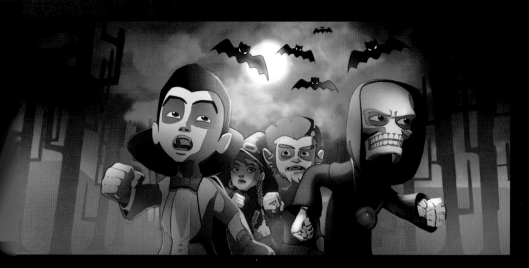

o take on terrifying teachers and homework horrors,
hey formed the most fearsome friendship on Earth . . .

Mighty Mighty MONSTERS

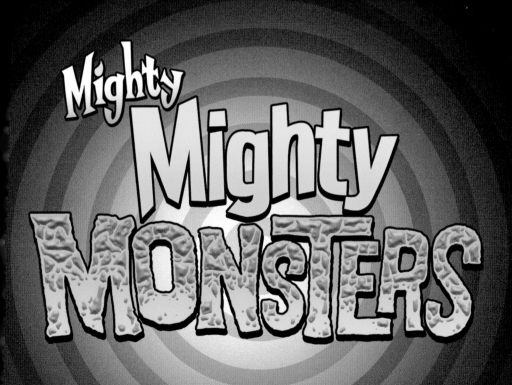

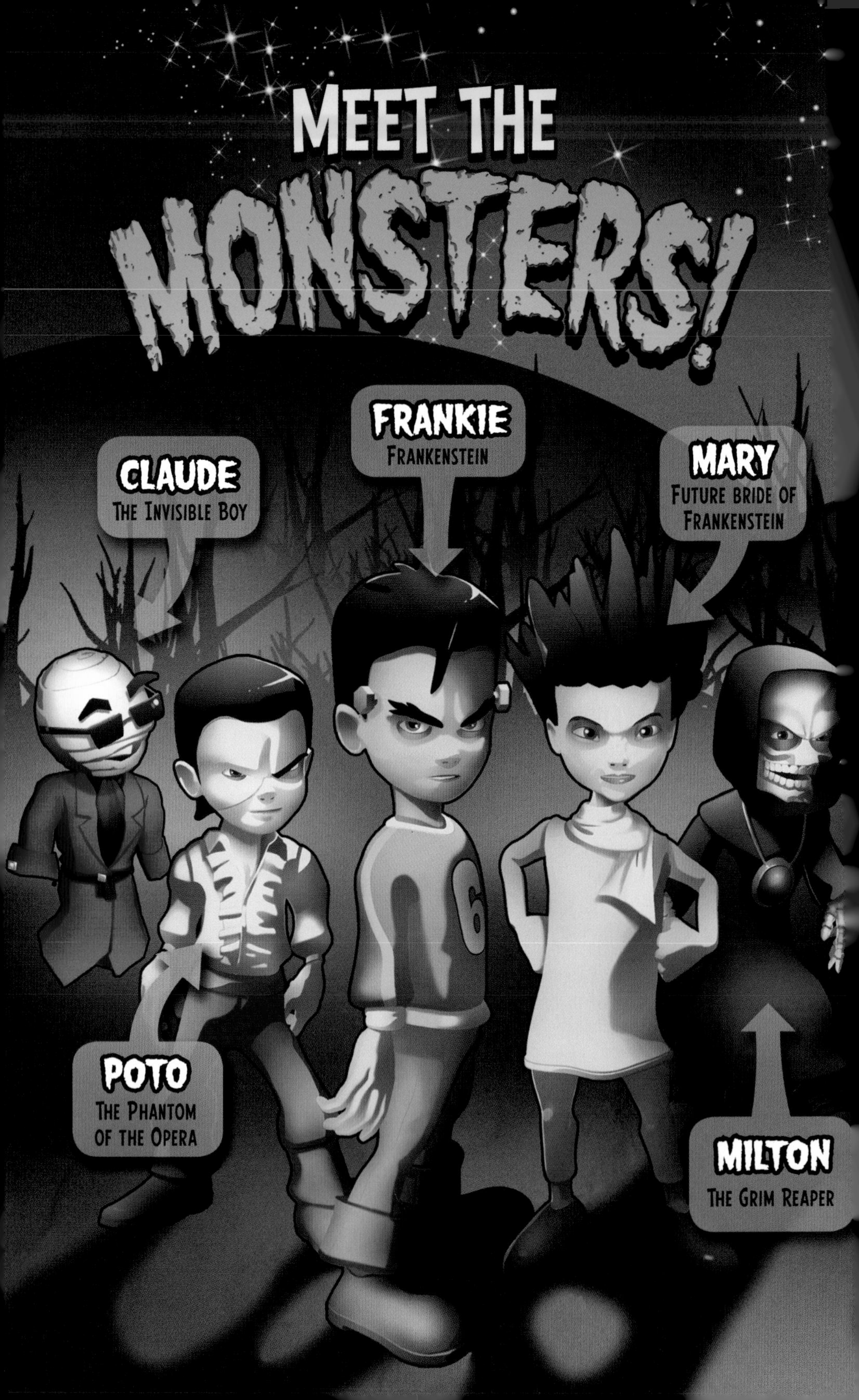
MEET THE
MONSTERS!
FRANKIE
FRANKENSTEIN
CLAUDE
THE INVISIBLE BOY
MARY
FUTURE BRIDE OF FRANKENSTEIN
POTO
THE PHANTOM OF THE OPERA
MILTON
THE GRIM REAPER

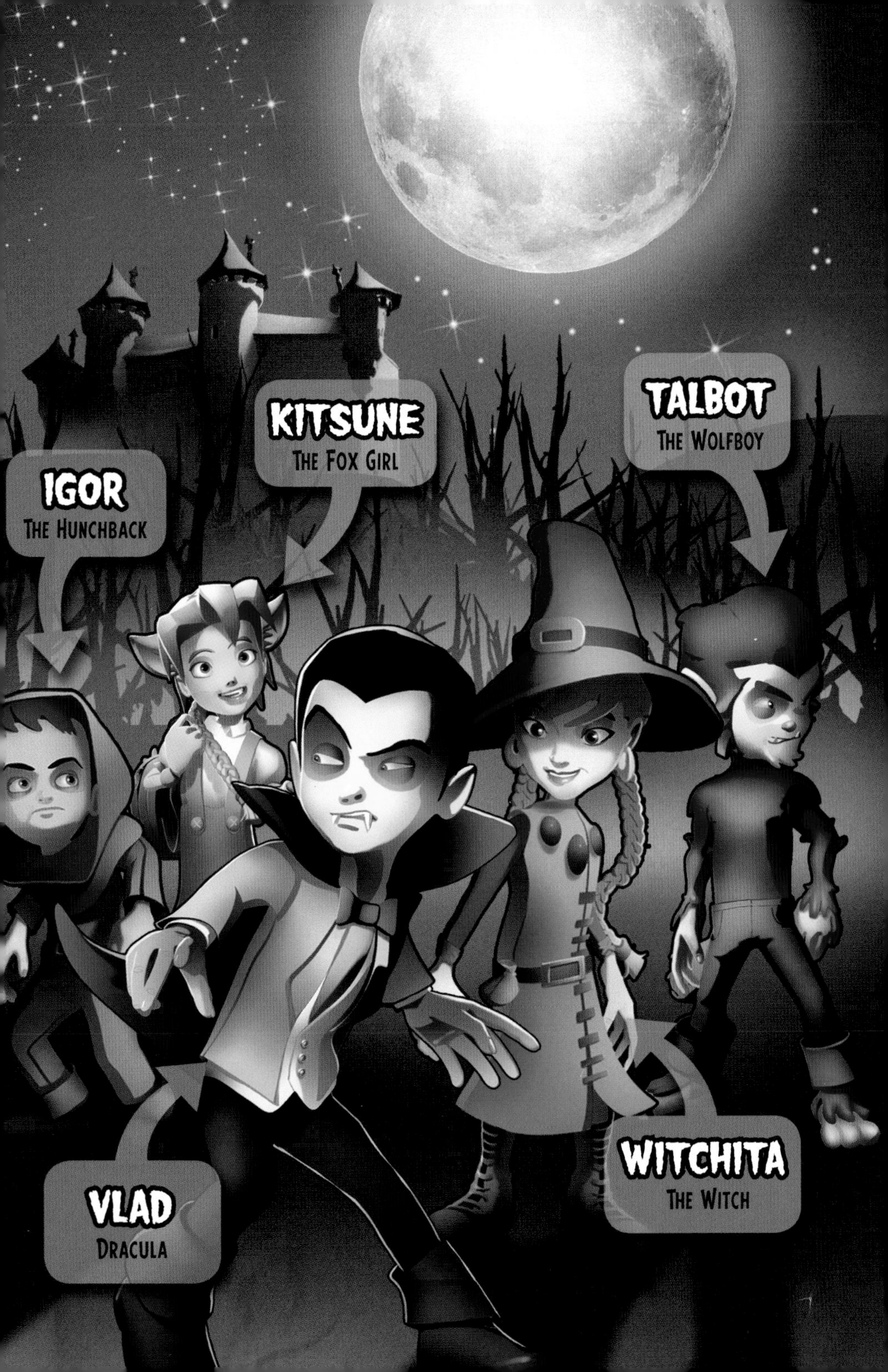
KITSUNE
THE FOX GIRL
TALBOT
THE WOLFBOY
IGOR
THE HUNCHBACK
WITCHITA
THE WITCH
VLAD
DRACULA

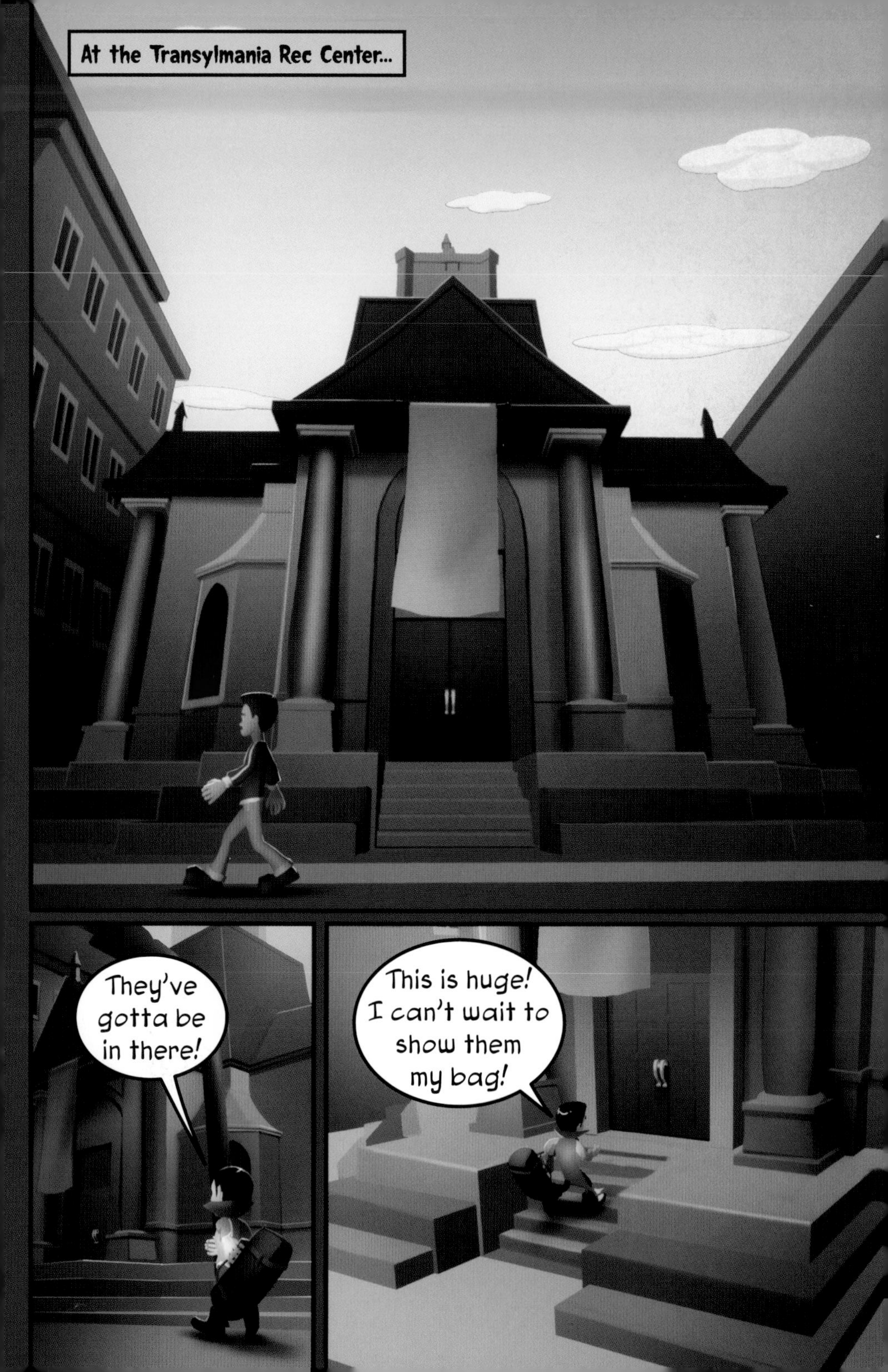
At the Transylmania Rec Center...
They've gotta be in there!
This is huge! I can't wait to show them my bag!

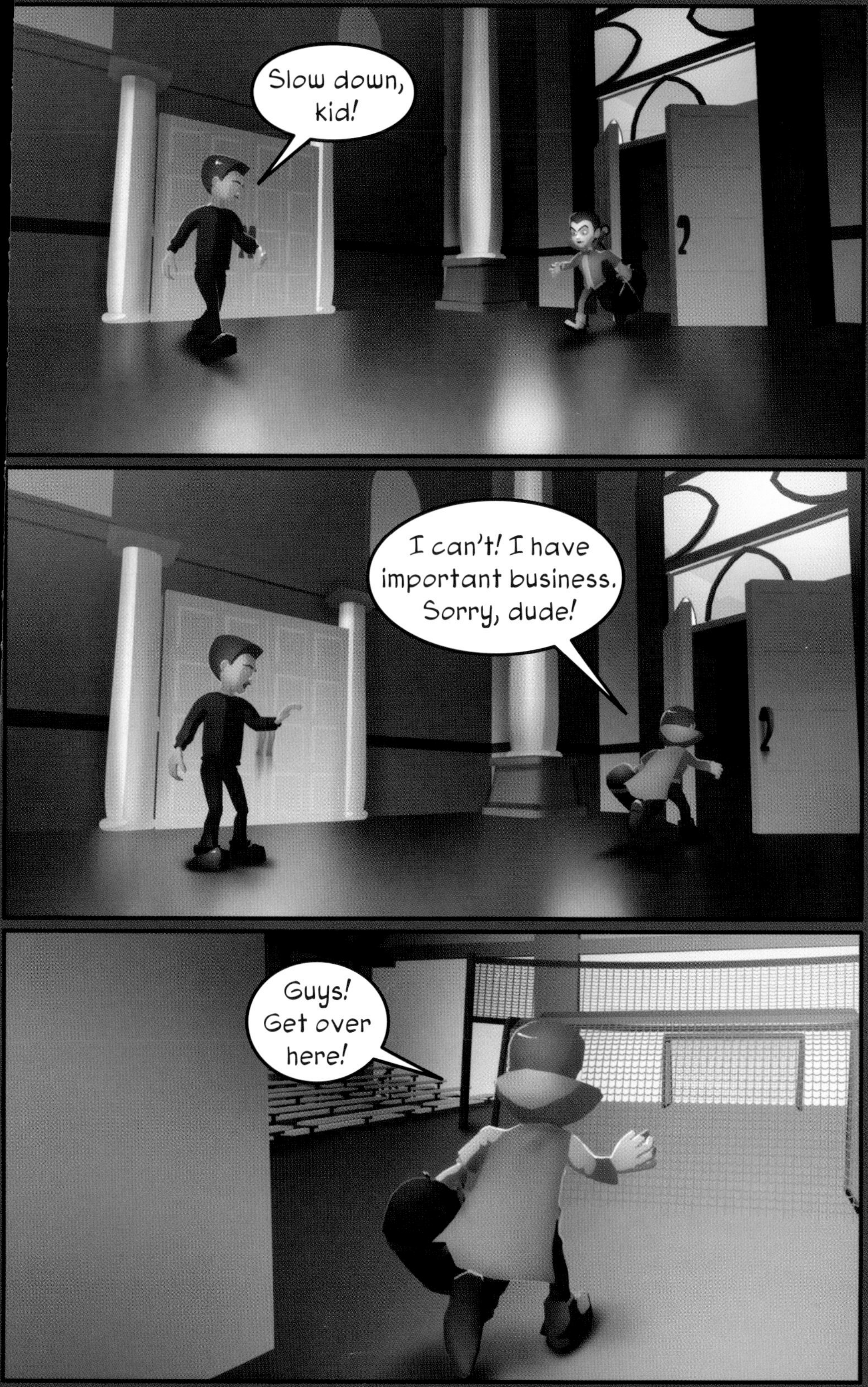
Slow down, kid!
I can't! I have important business. Sorry, dude!
Guys! Get over here!

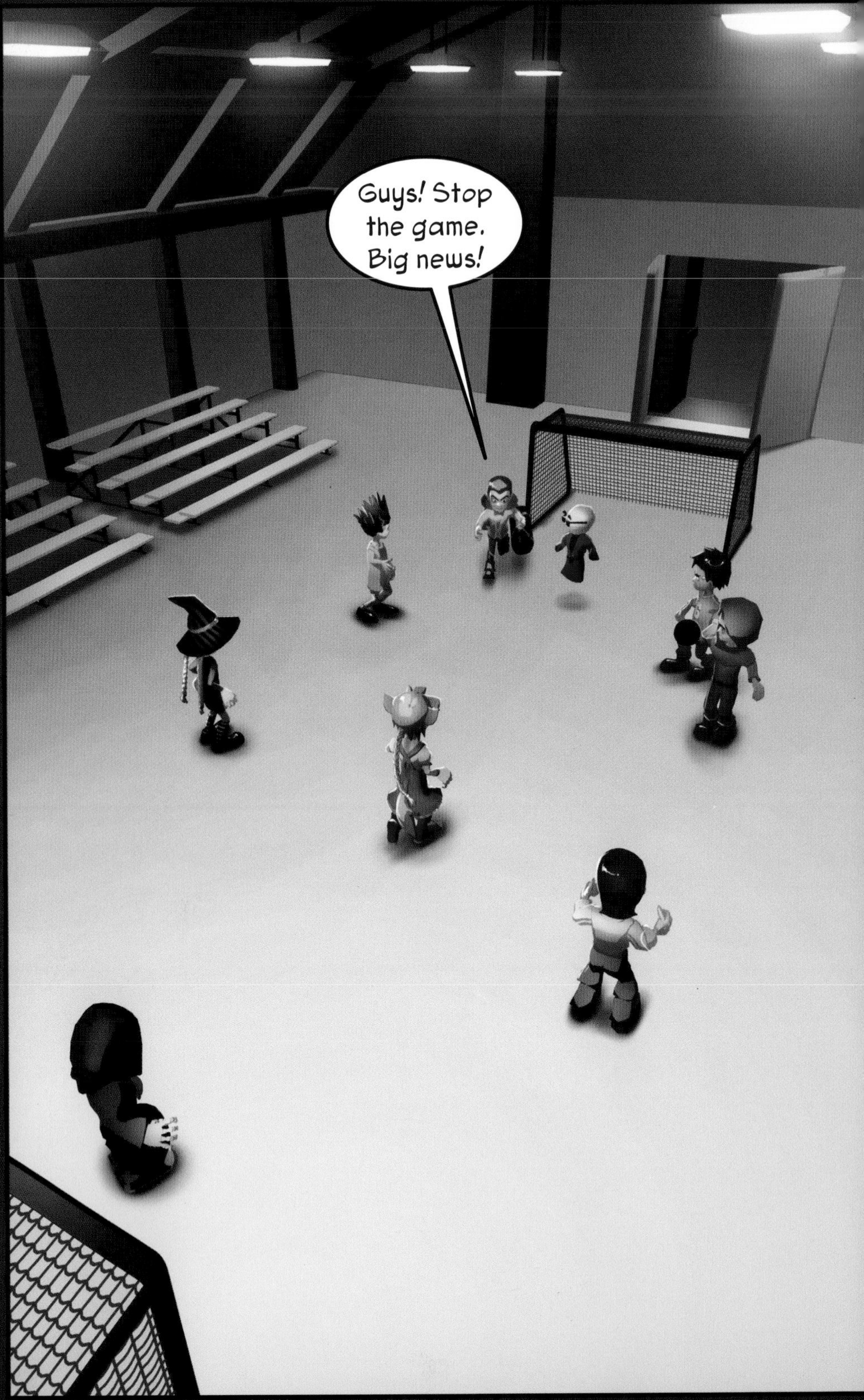
Guys! Stop the game. Big news!

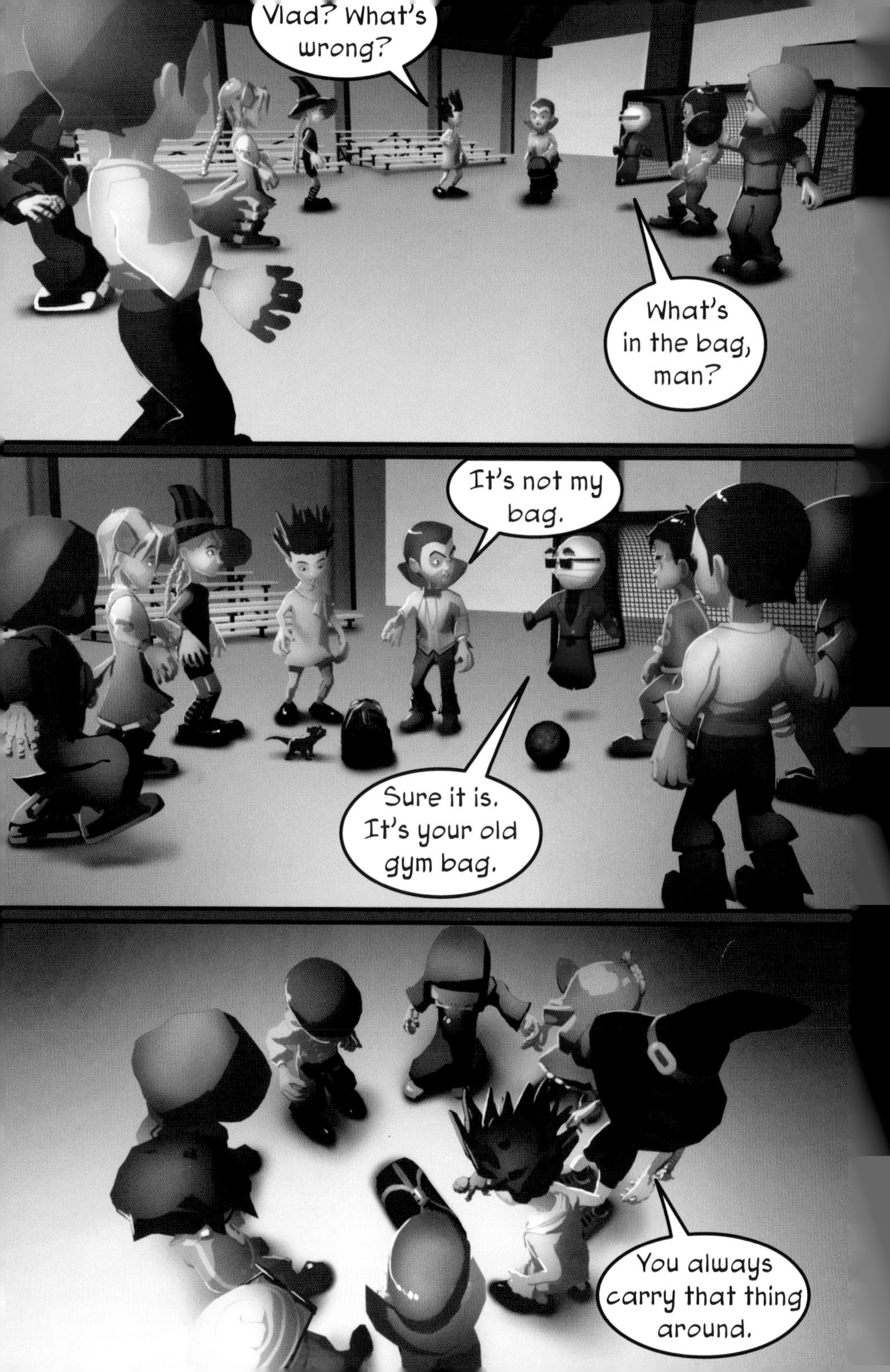
Vlad? What's wrong?
What's in the bag, man?
It's not my bag.
Sure it is. It's your old gym bag.
You always carry that thing around.

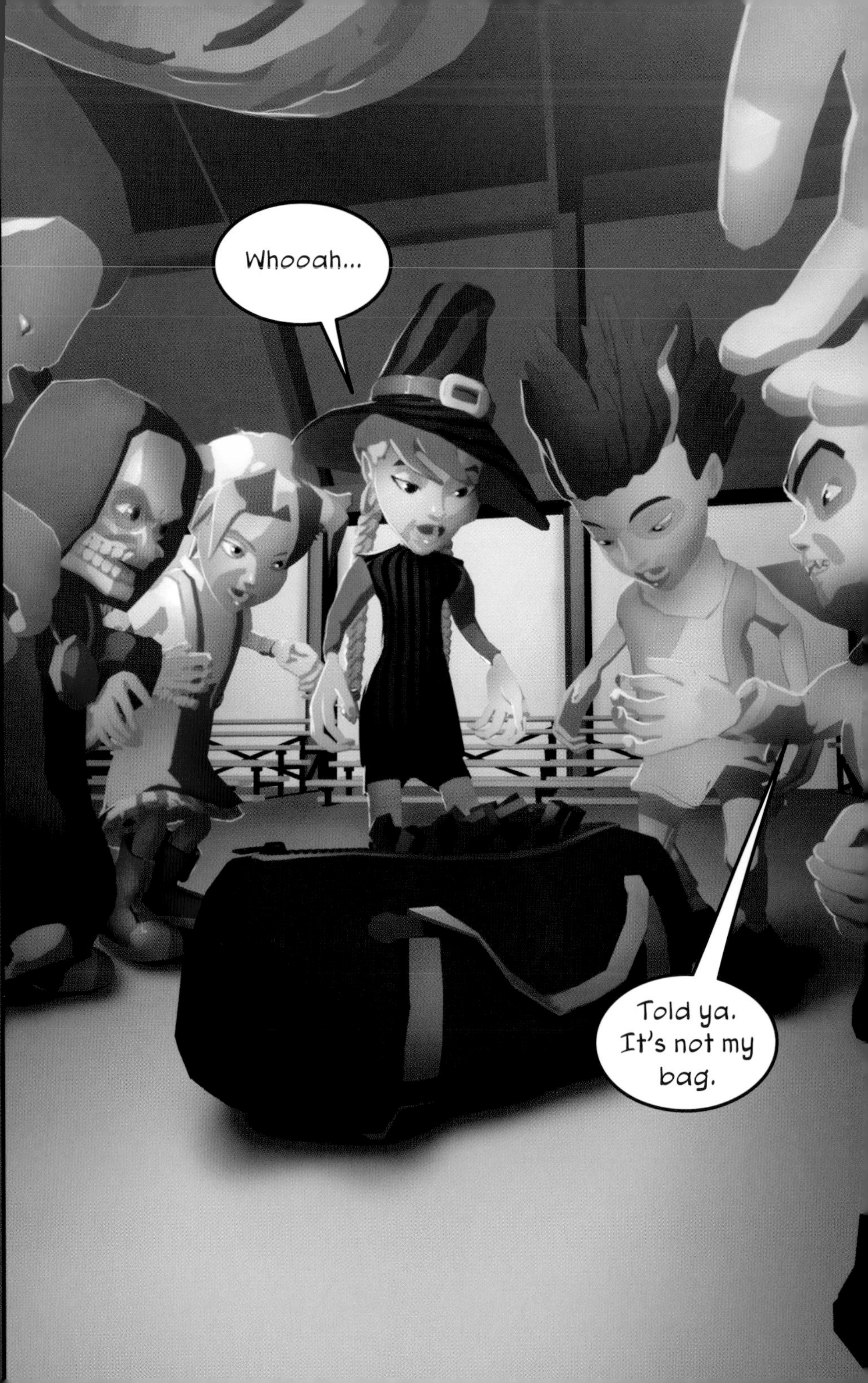
Whooah...
Told ya. It's not my bag.

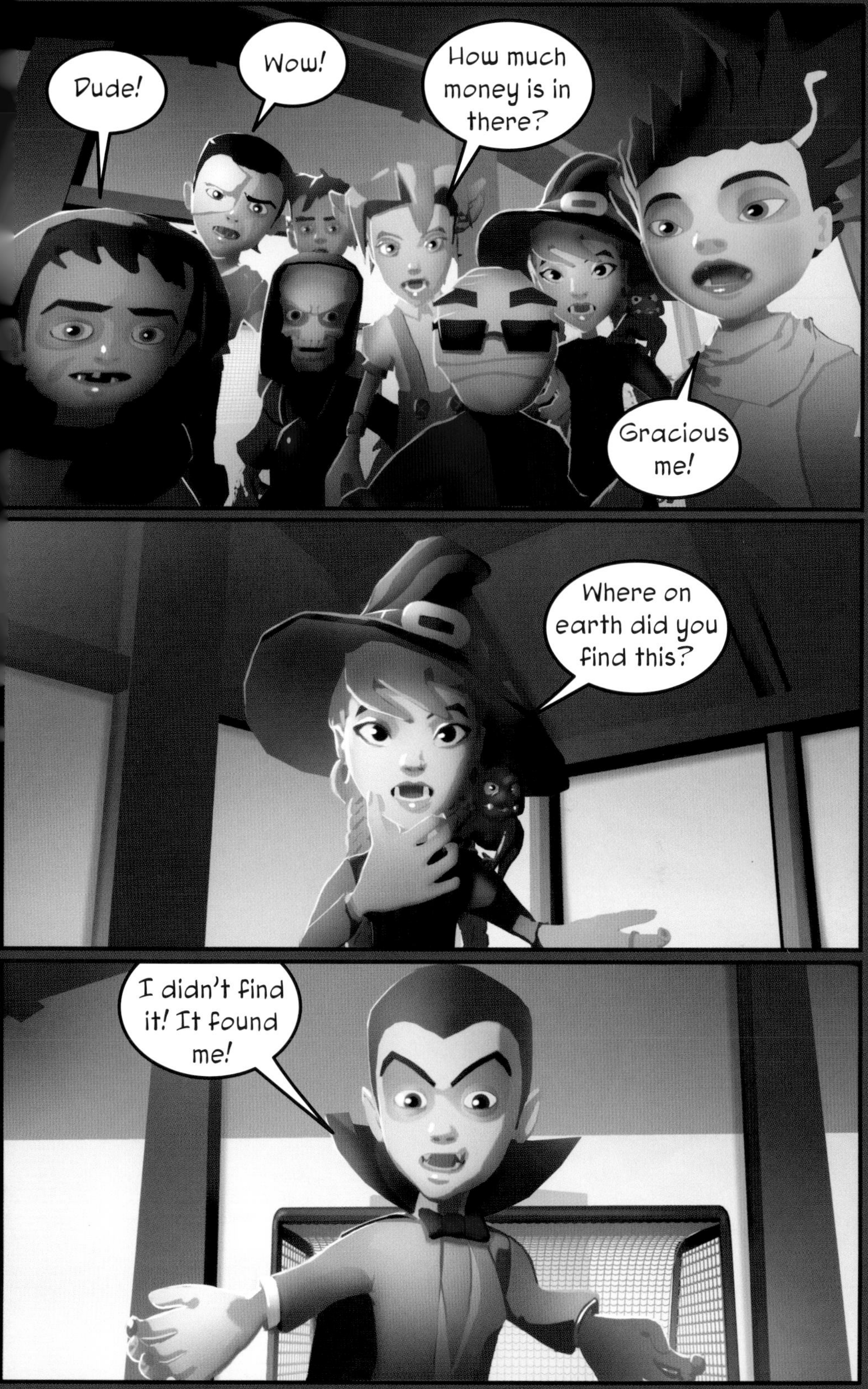
Dude!
Wow!
How much money is in there?
Gracious me!
Where on earth did you find this?
I didn't find it! It found me!

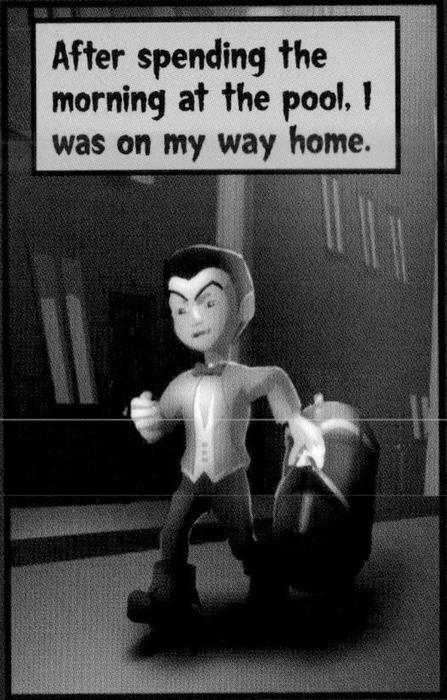
After spending the morning at the pool, I was on my way home.

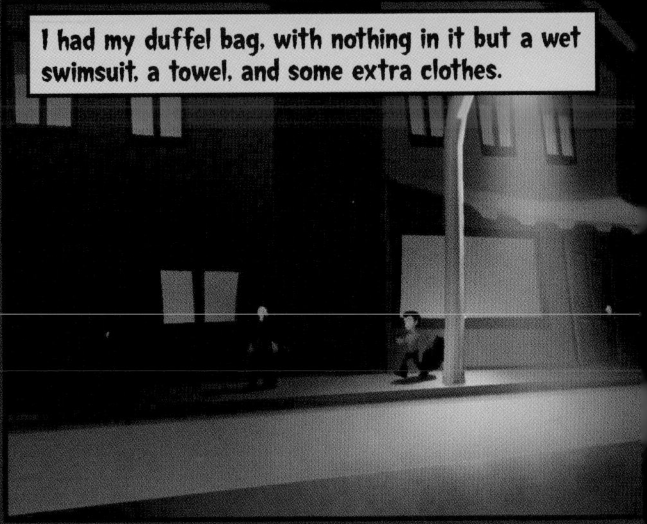
I had my duffel bag, with nothing in it but a wet swimsuit, a towel, and some extra clothes.

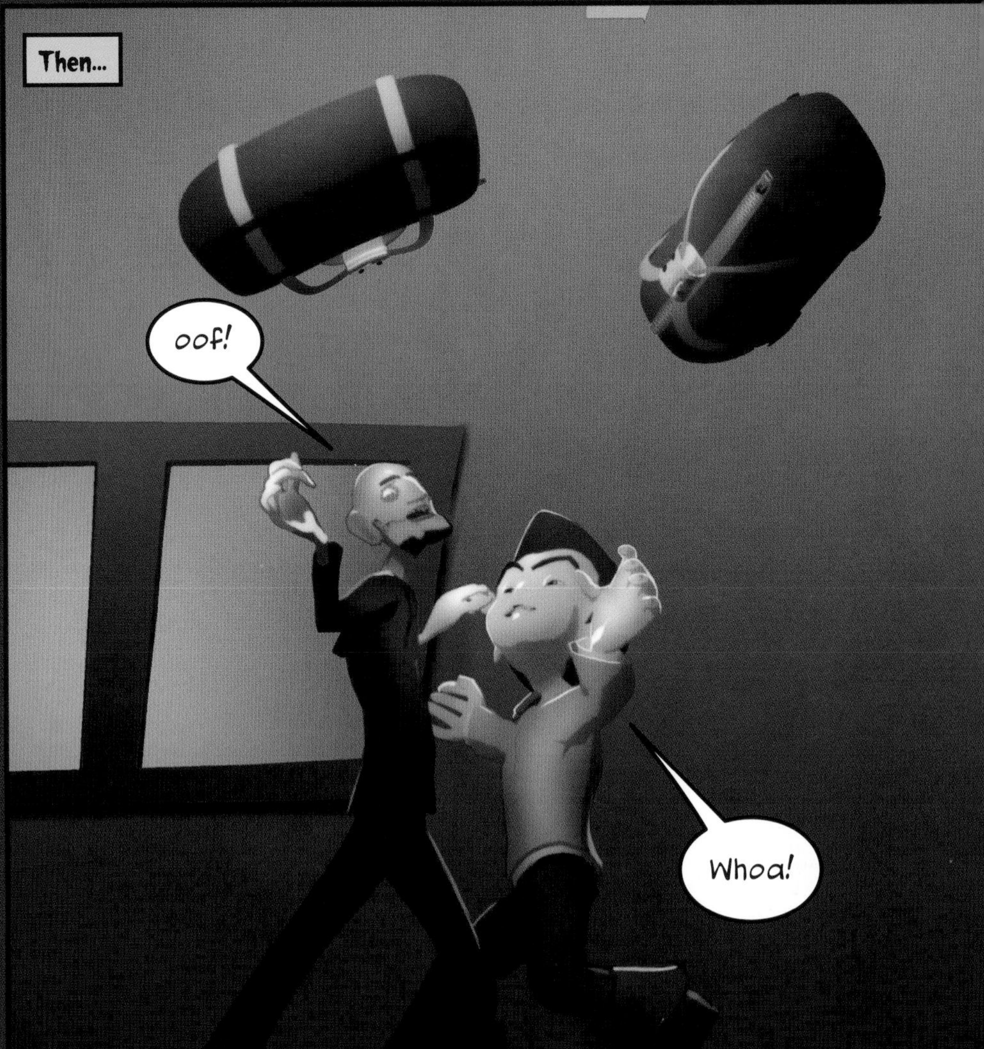
Then...
oof!
Whoa!

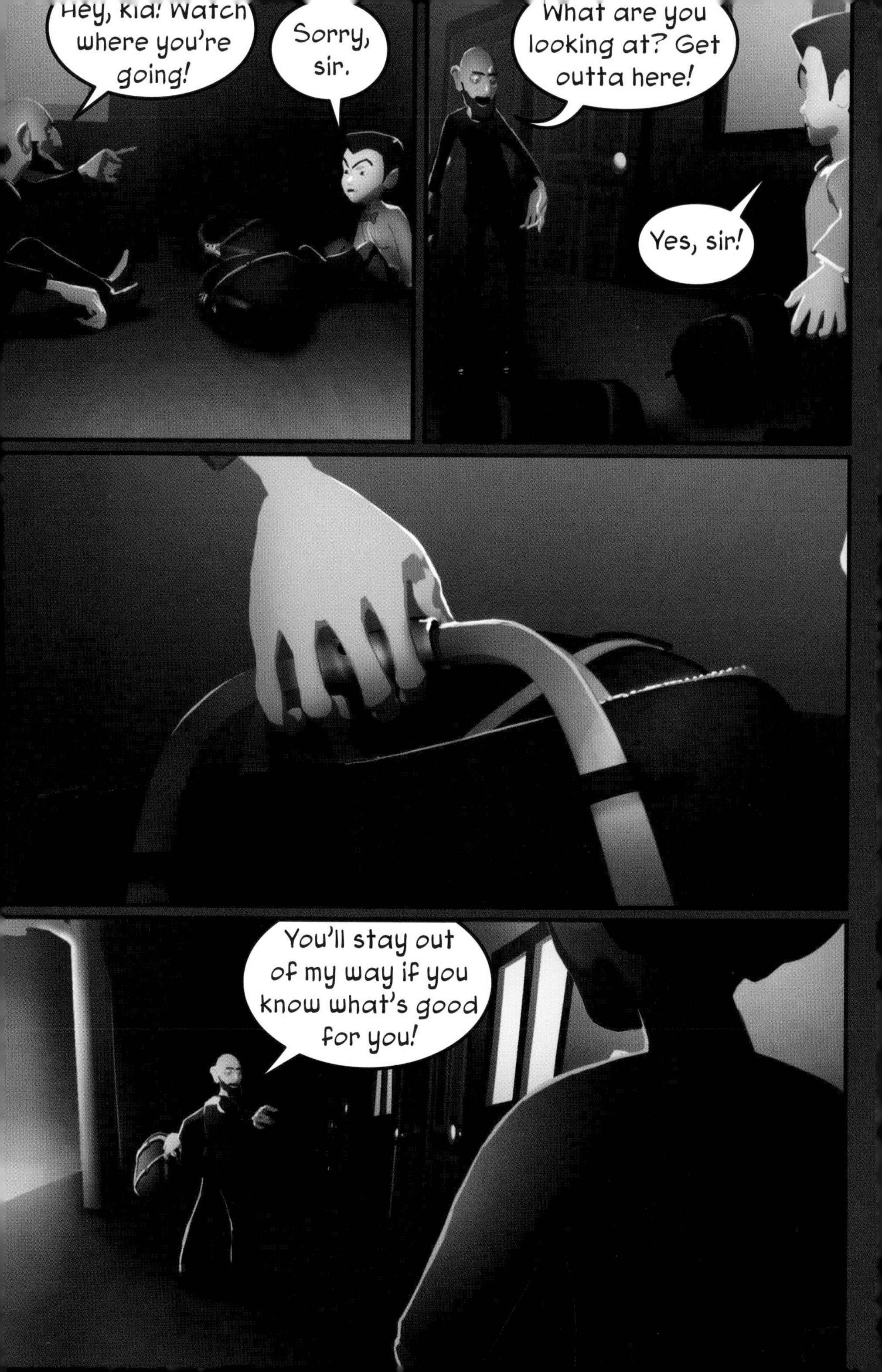
Hey, kid! Watch where you're going!
Sorry, sir.
What are you looking at? Get outta here!
Yes, sir!
You'll stay out of my way if you know what's good for you!

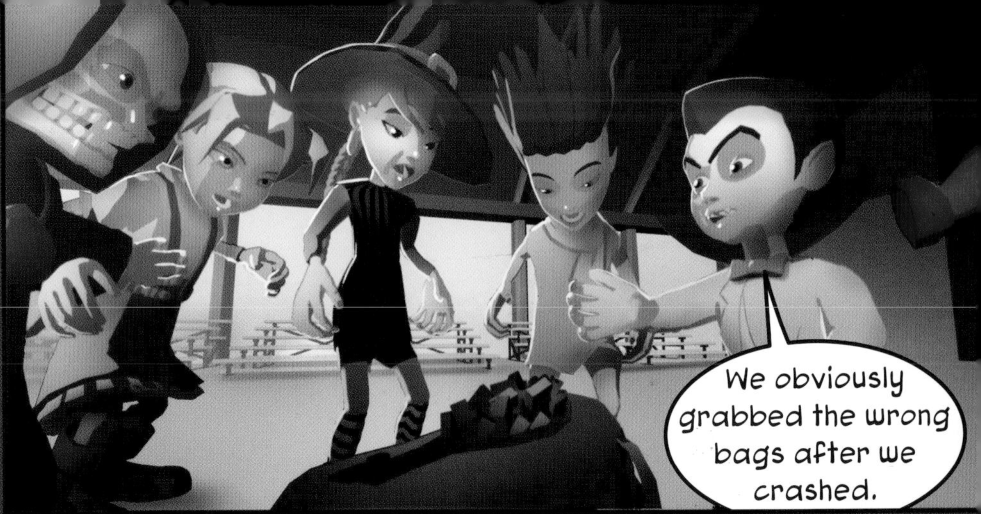
We obviously grabbed the wrong bags after we crashed.

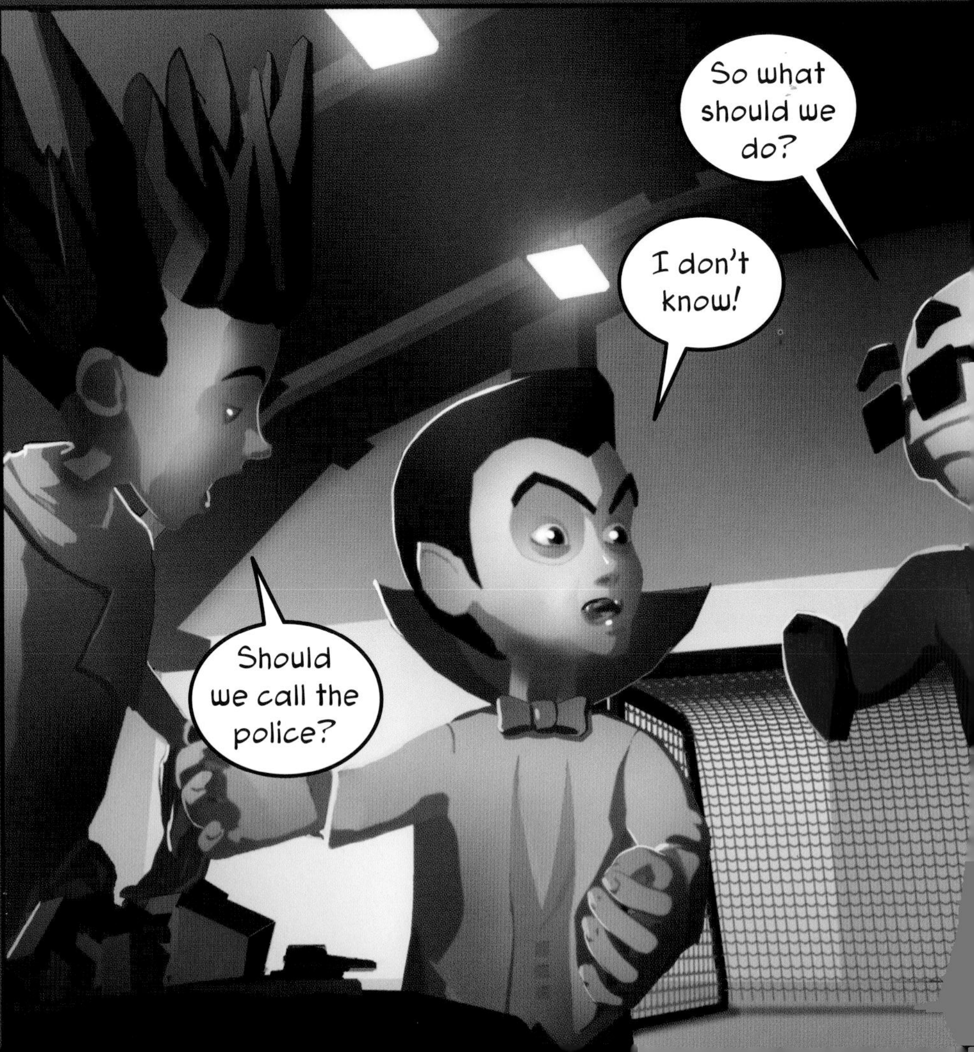
So what should we do?
I don't know!
Should we call the police?

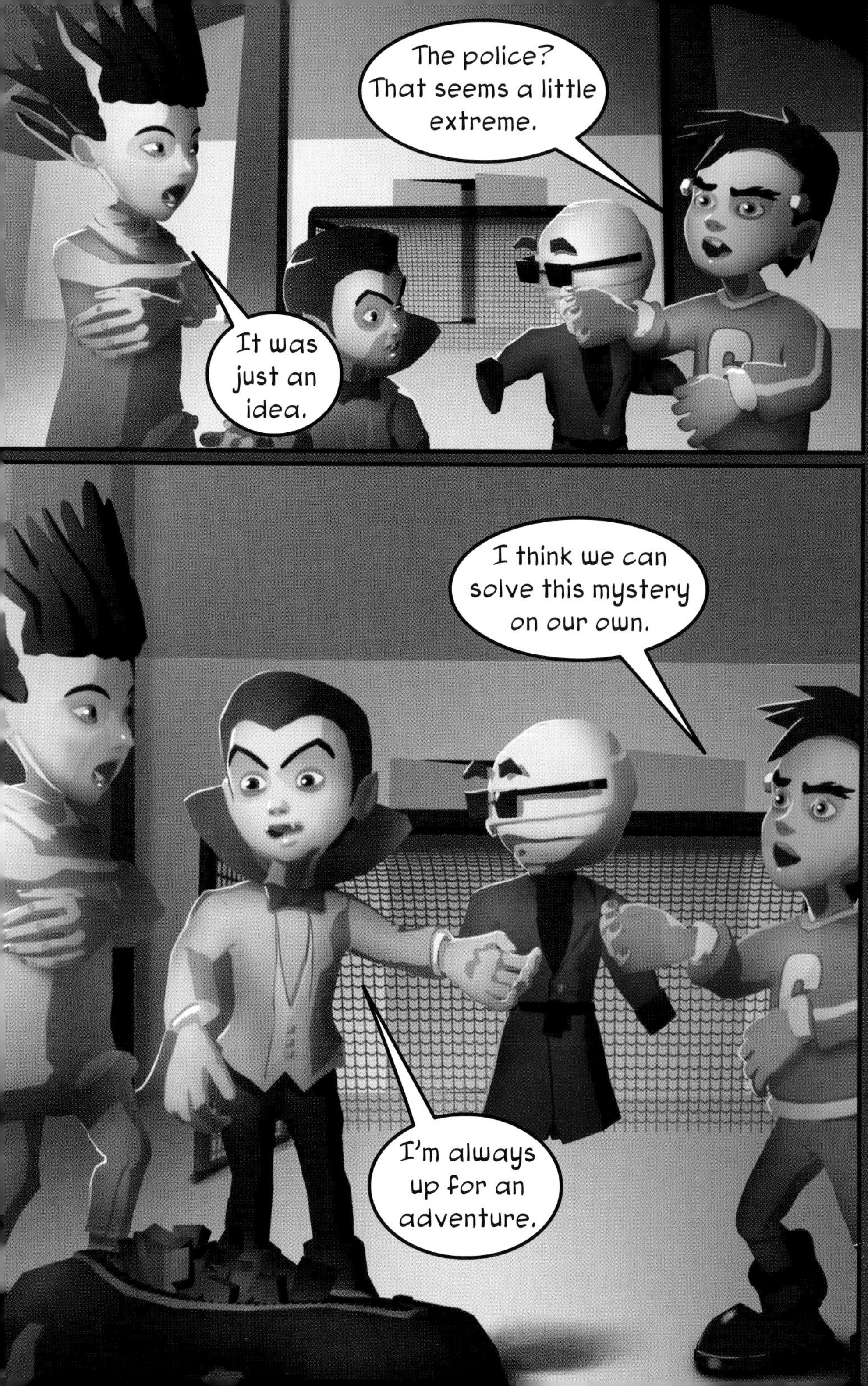
The police? That seems a little extreme.
It was just an idea.
I think we can solve this mystery on our own.
I'm always up for an adventure.

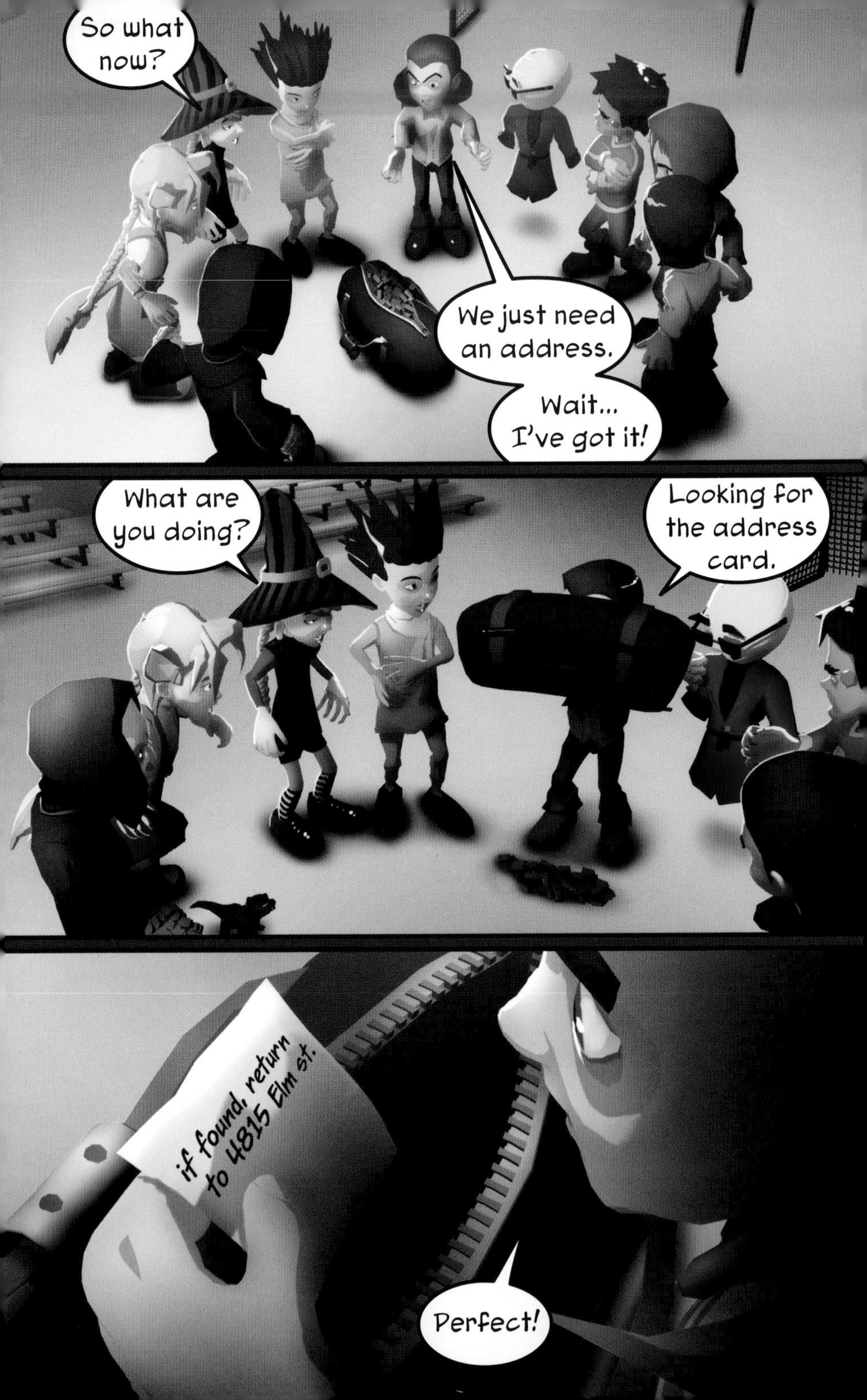
So what now?
We just need an address.
Wait... I've got it!
What are you doing?
Looking for the address card.
if found, return to 4815 Elm st.
Perfect!

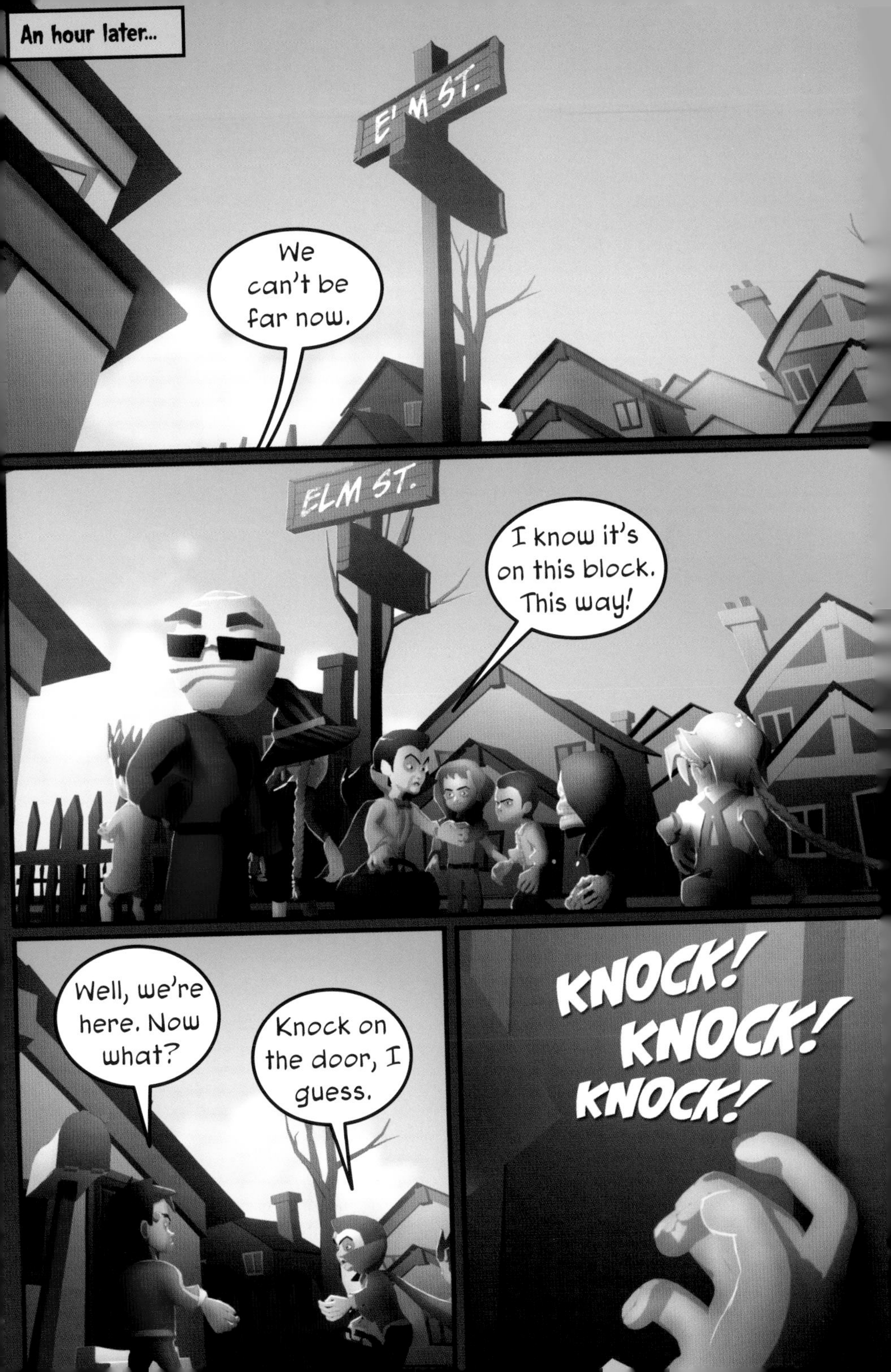

An hour later...
ELM ST.
We can't be far now.
ELM ST.
I know it's on this block. This way!
Well, we're here. Now what?
Knock on the door, I guess.
KNOCK! KNOCK! KNOCK!

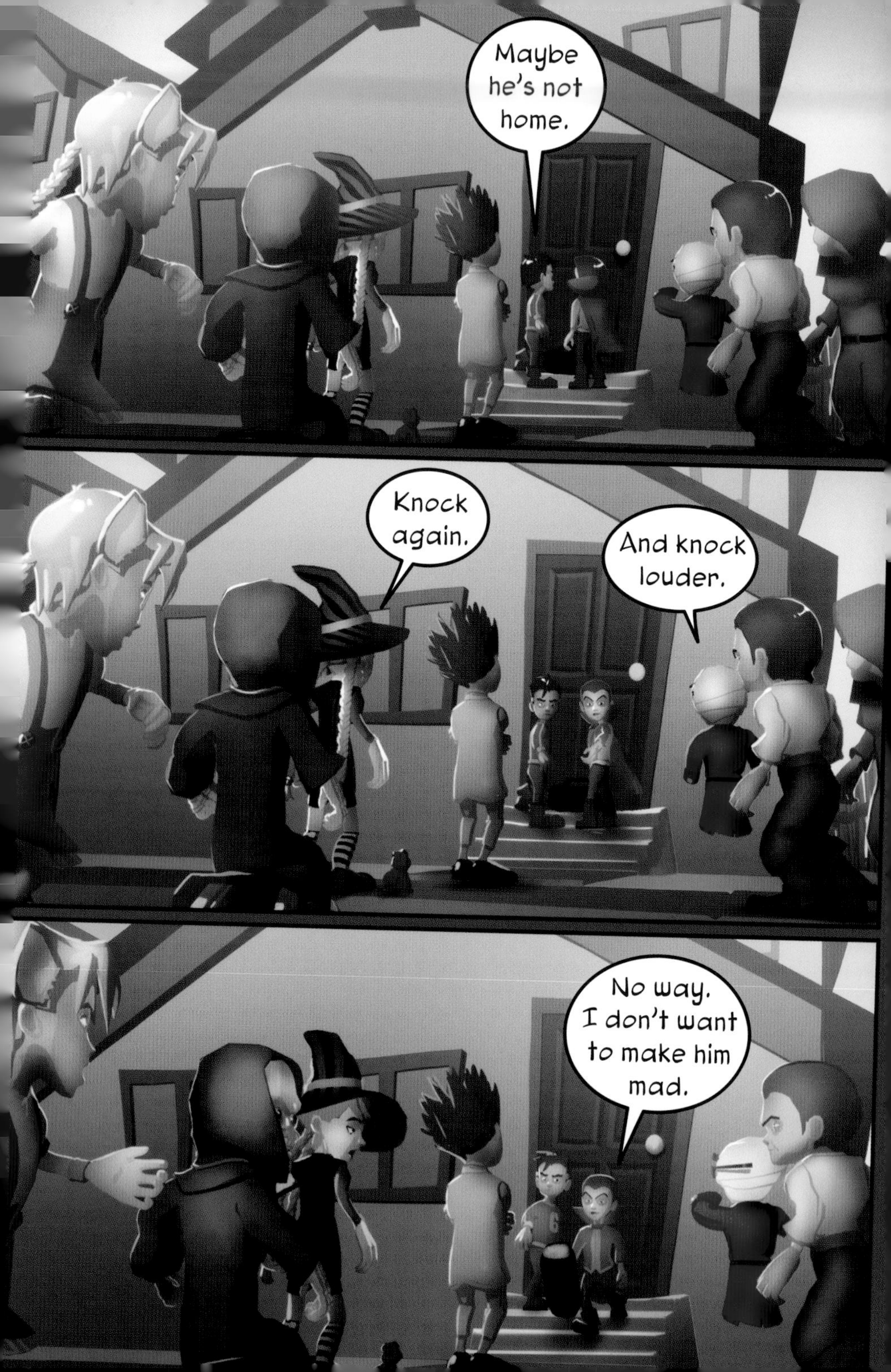
Maybe he's not home.
Knock again.
And knock louder.
No way. I don't want to make him mad.

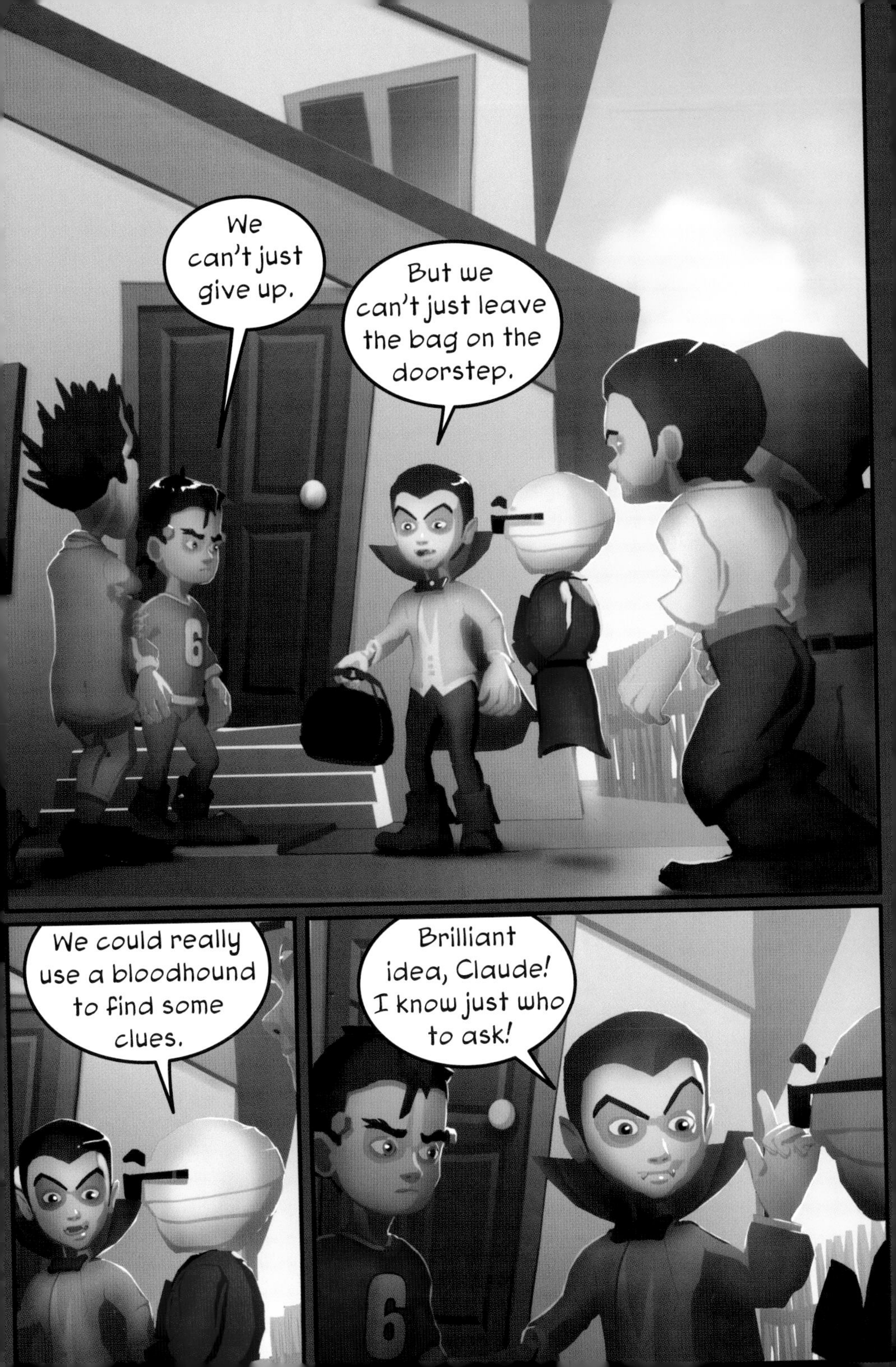
We can't just give up.
But we can't just leave the bag on the doorstep.
We could really use a bloodhound to find some clues.
Brilliant idea, Claude! I know just who to ask!

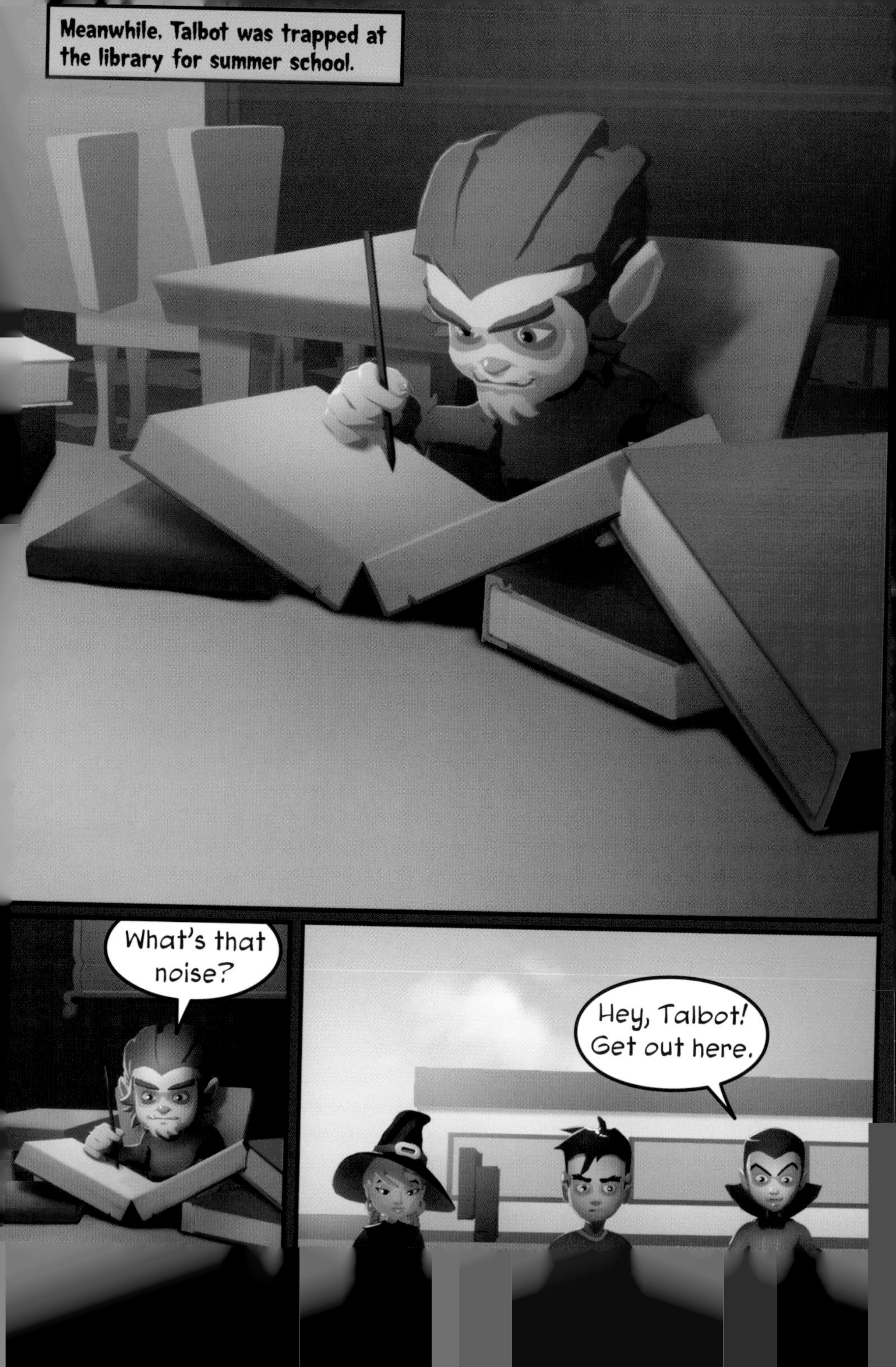
Meanwhile, Talbot was trapped at the library for summer school.
What's that noise?
Hey, Talbot! Get out here.

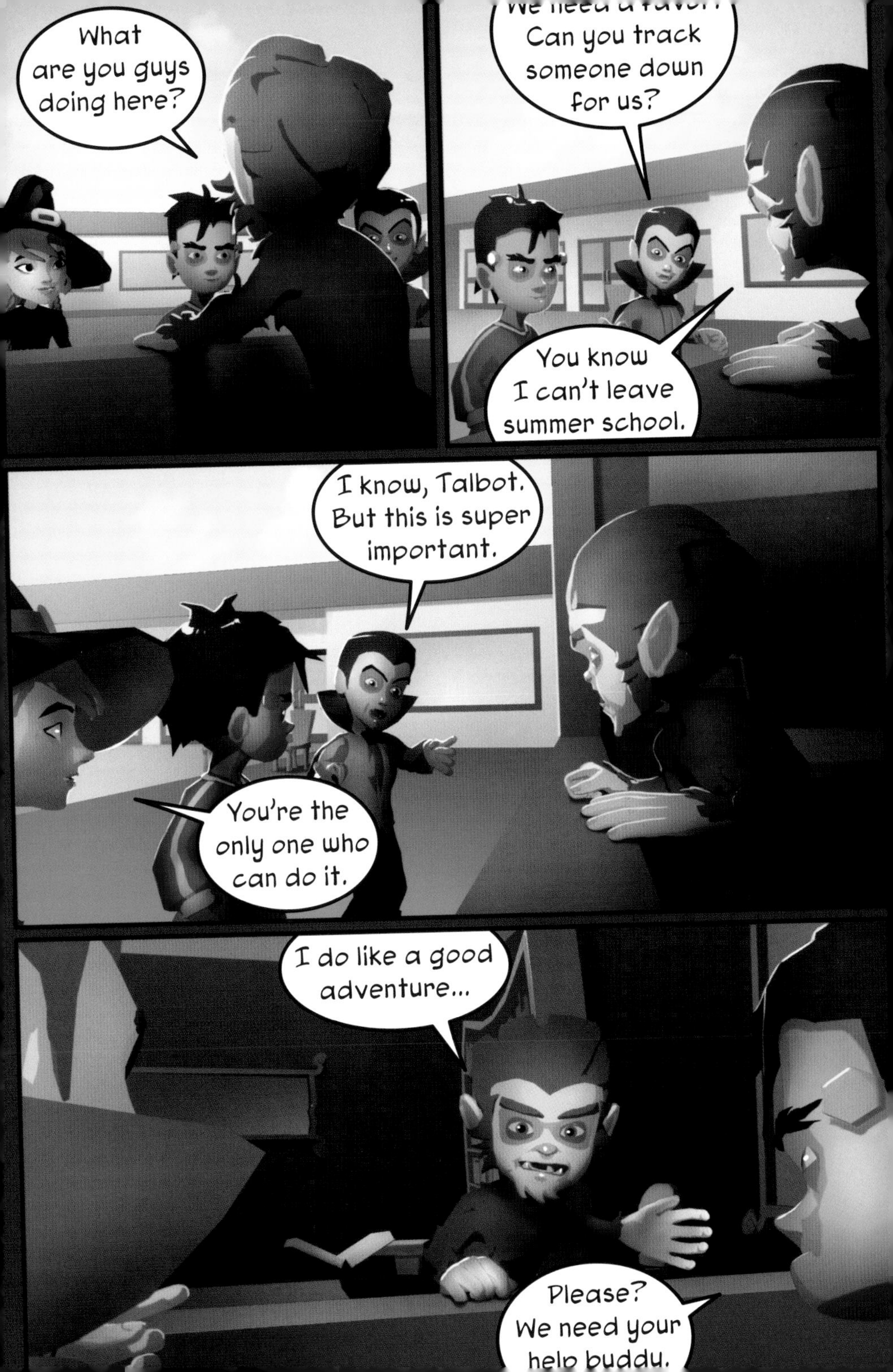
What are you guys doing here?
Can you track someone down for us?
You know I can't leave summer school.
I know, Talbot. But this is super important.
You're the only one who can do it.
I do like a good adventure...
Please? We need your help buddy.

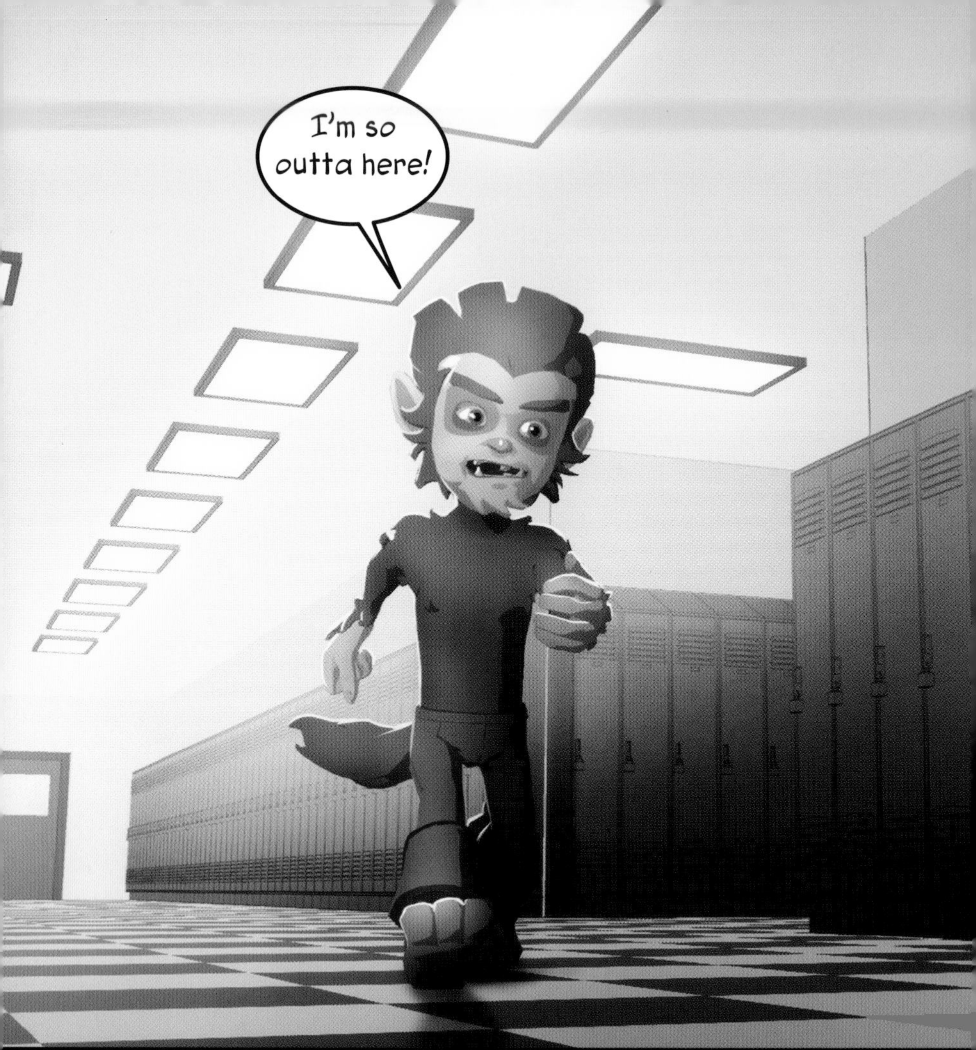
I'm so outta here!

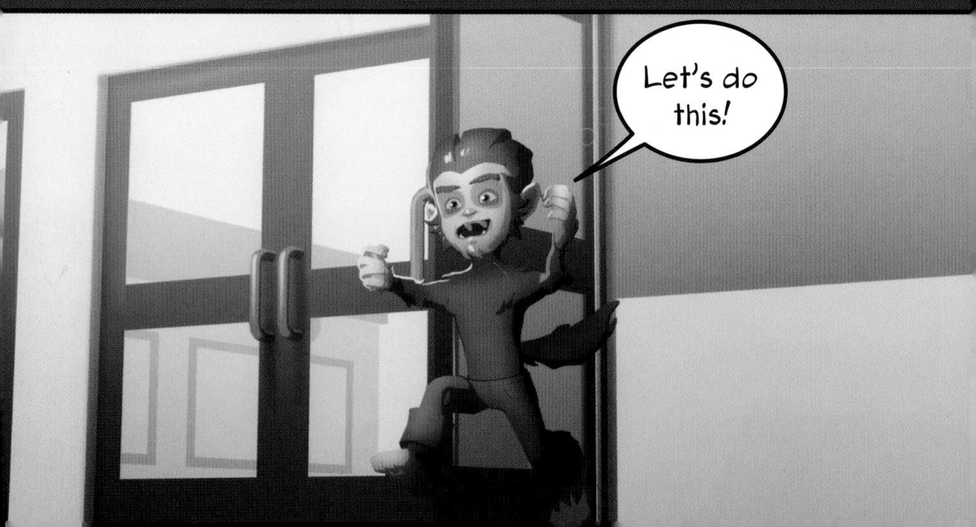
Let's do this!

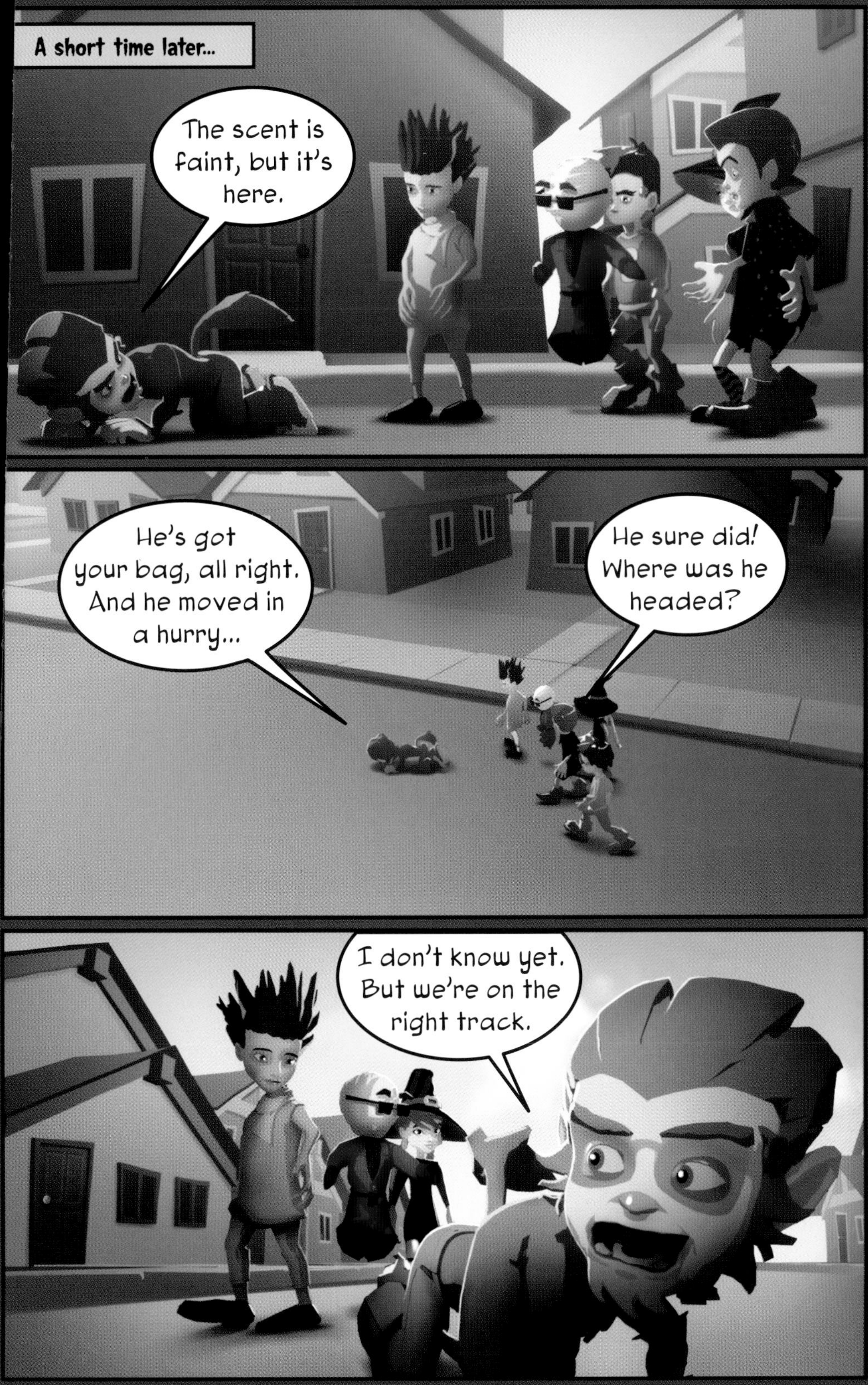
A short time later...
The scent is faint, but it's here.
He's got your bag, all right. And he moved in a hurry...
He sure did! Where was he headed?
I don't know yet. But we're on the right track.

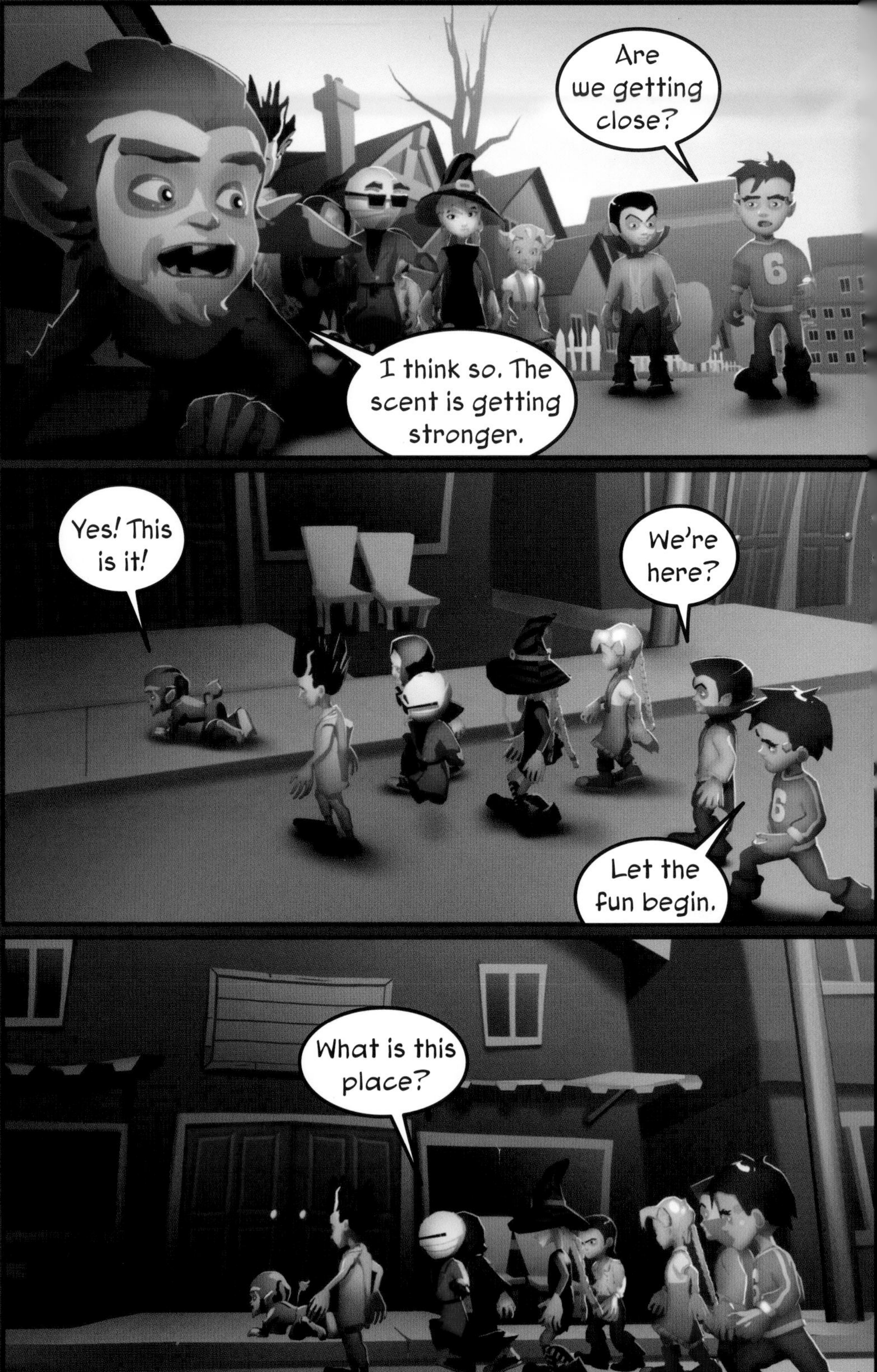
Are we getting close?
I think so. The scent is getting stronger.
Yes! This is it!
We're here?
Let the fun begin.
What is this place?

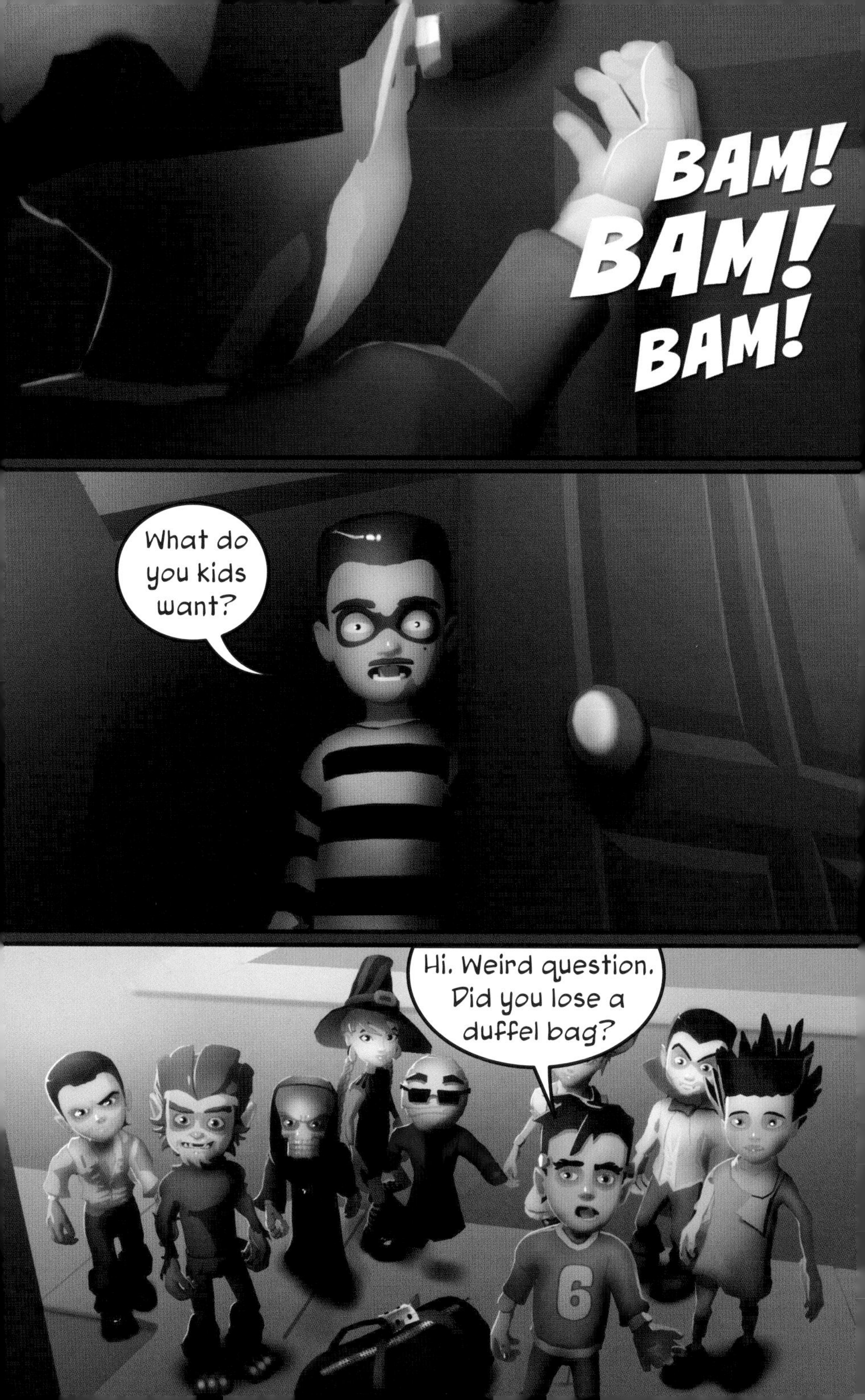
BAM!
BAM!
BAM!
What do you kids want?
Hi. Weird question. Did you lose a duffel bag?

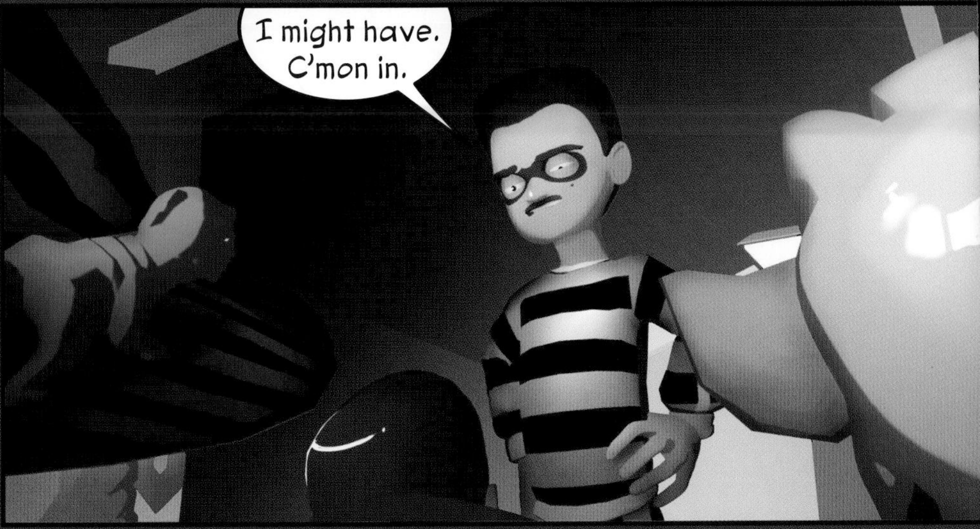
I might have. C'mon in.

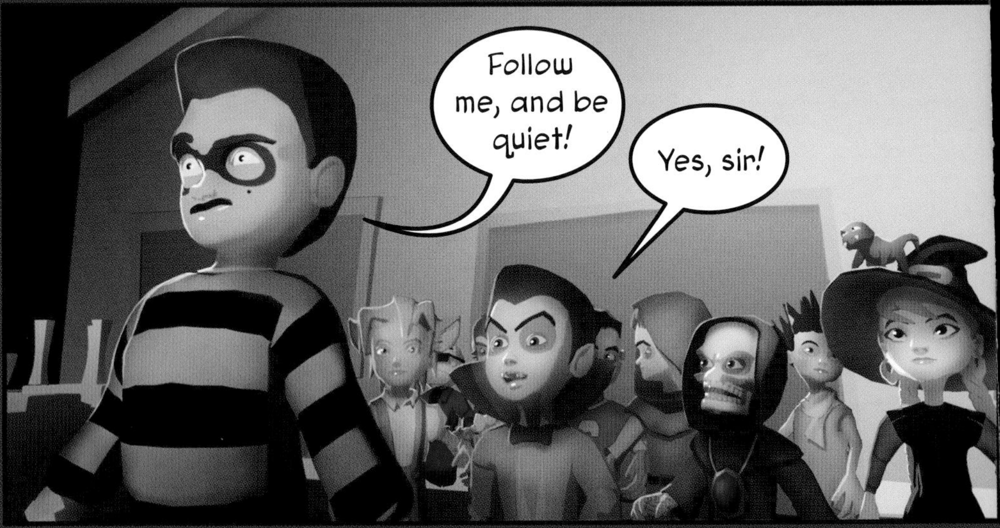
Follow me, and be quiet!
Yes, sir!

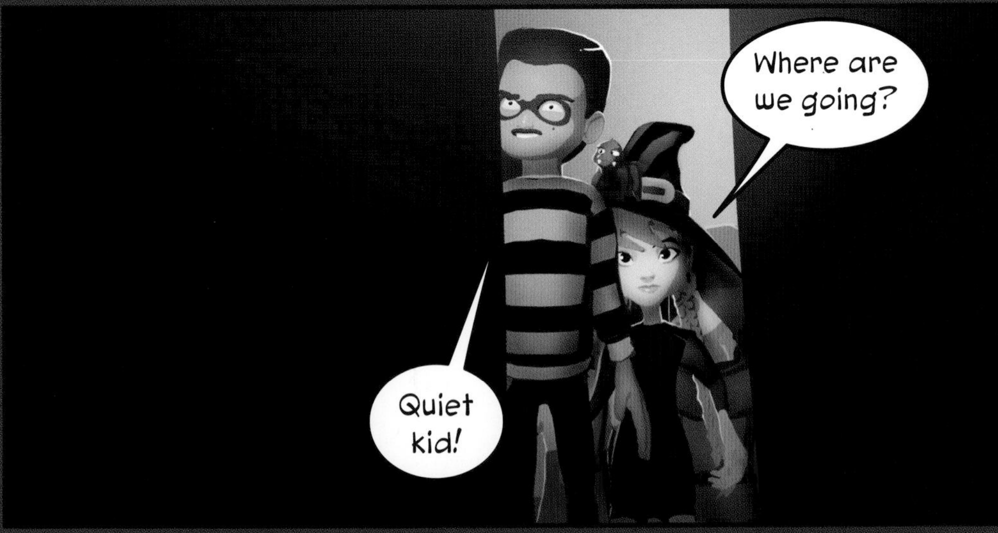
Where are we going?
Quiet kid!

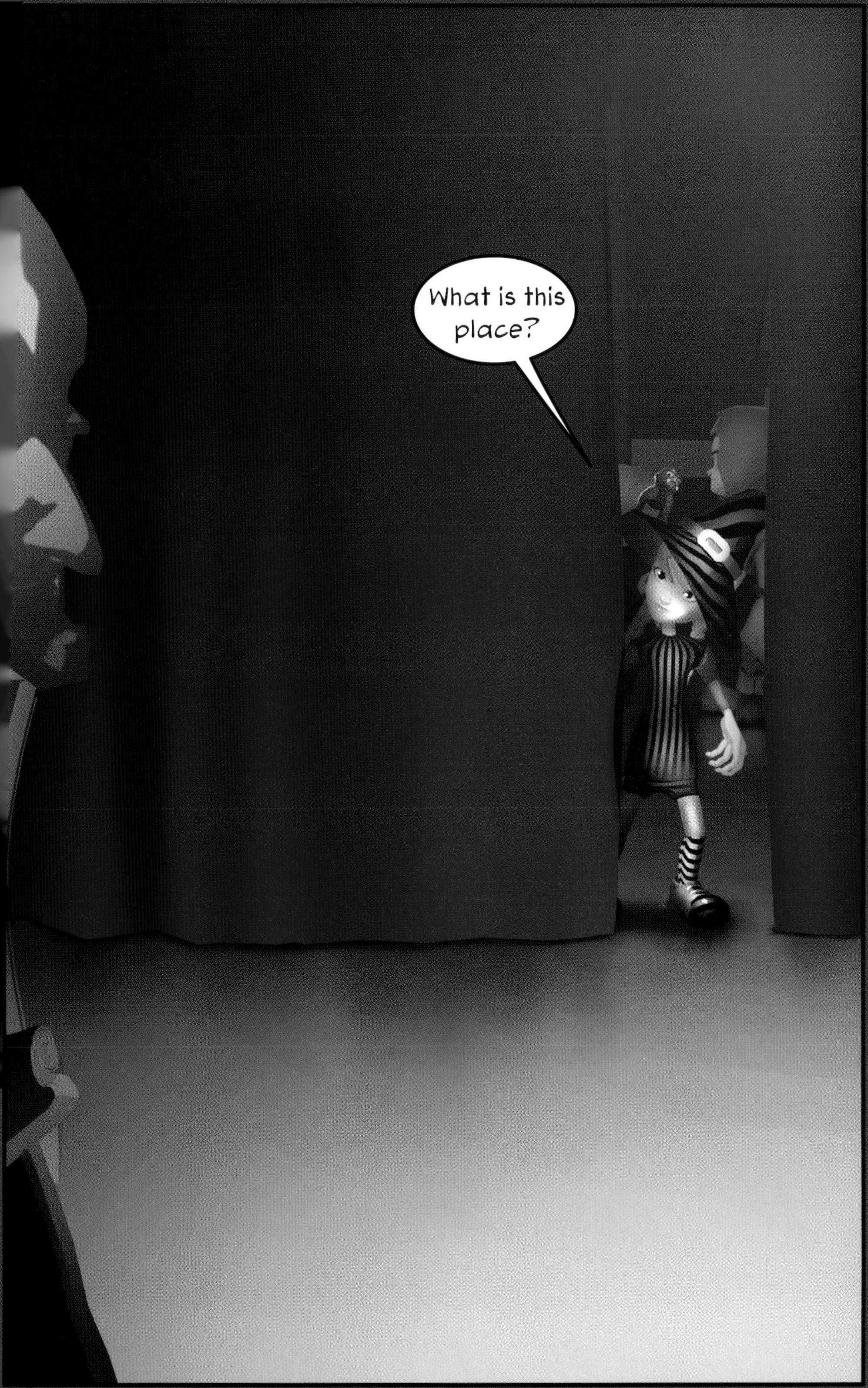
What is this place?

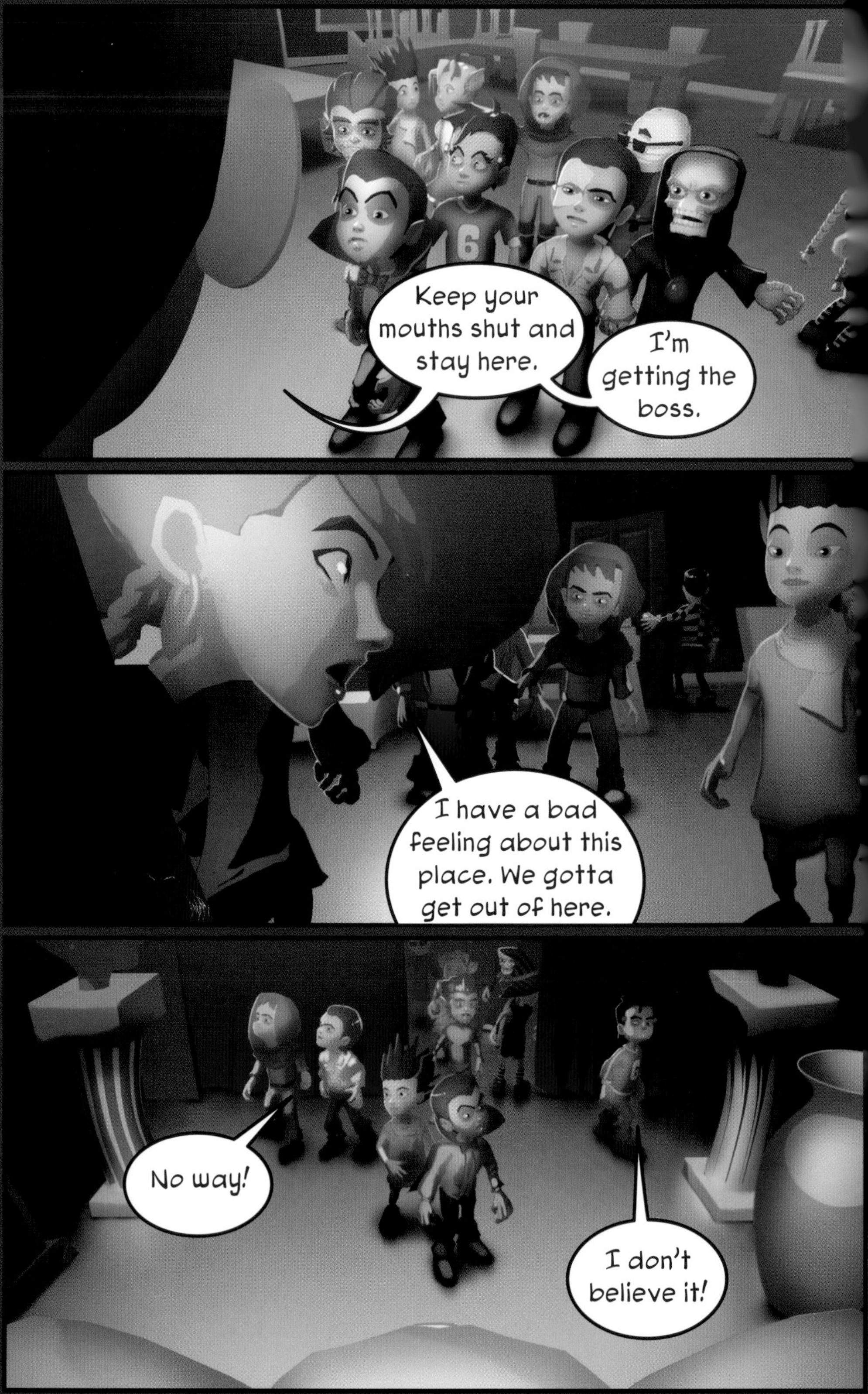
Keep your mouths shut and stay here.
I'm getting the boss.
I have a bad feeling about this place. We gotta get out of here.
No way!
I don't believe it!

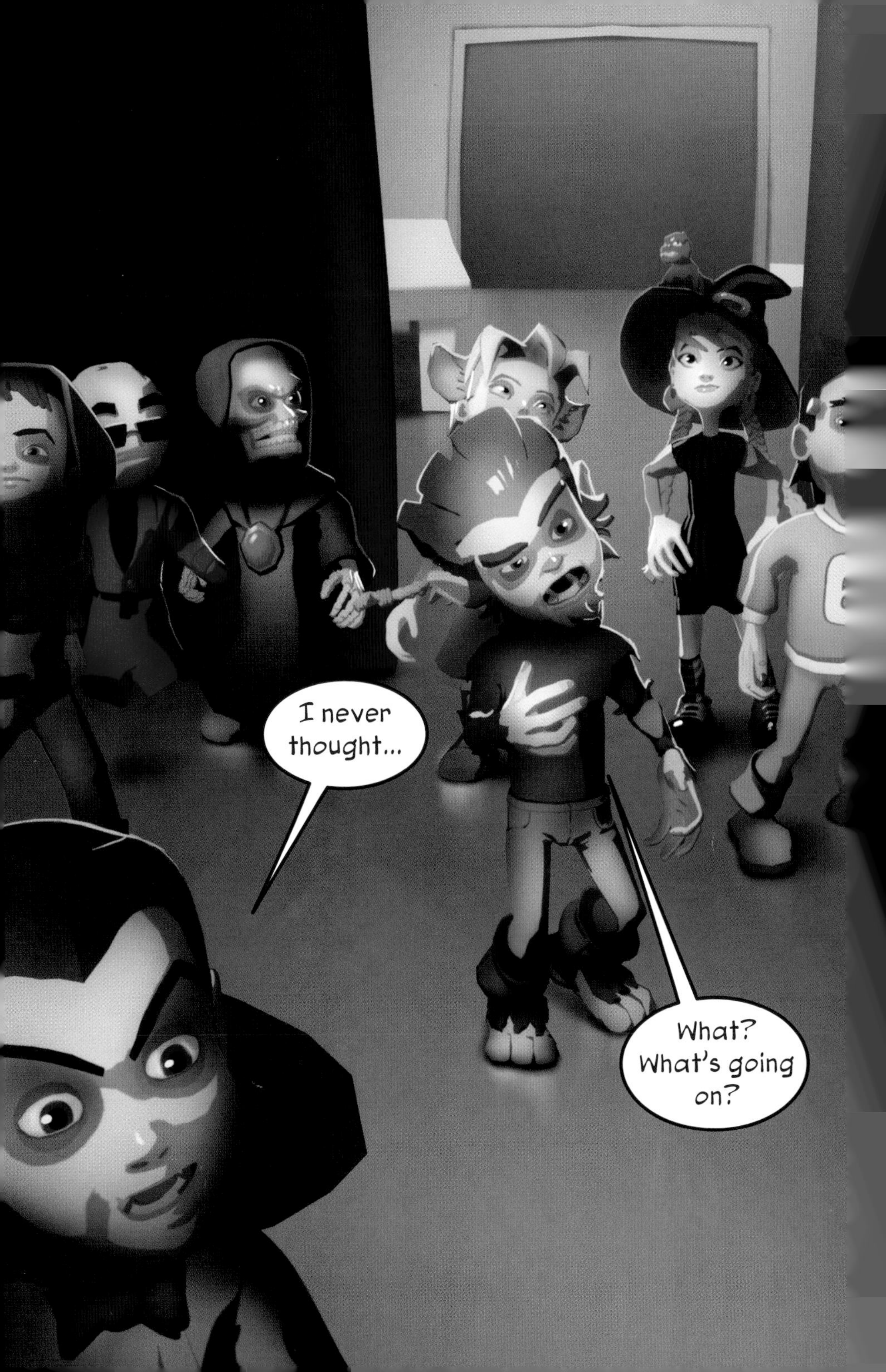
I never thought...
What? What's going on?

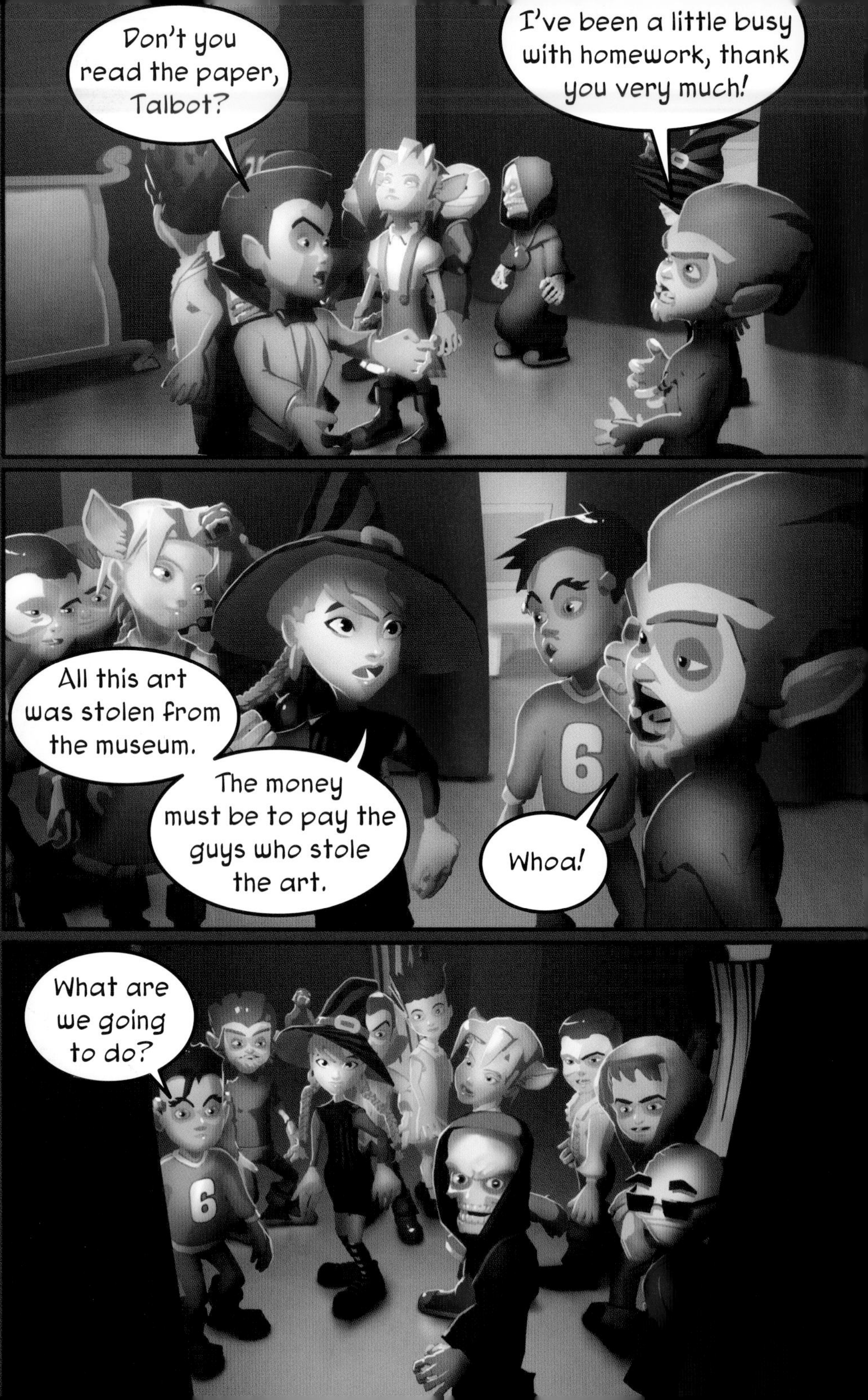
Don't you read the paper, Talbot?
I've been a little busy with homework, thank you very much!
All this art was stolen from the museum.
The money must be to pay the guys who stole the art.
Whoa!
What are we going to do?

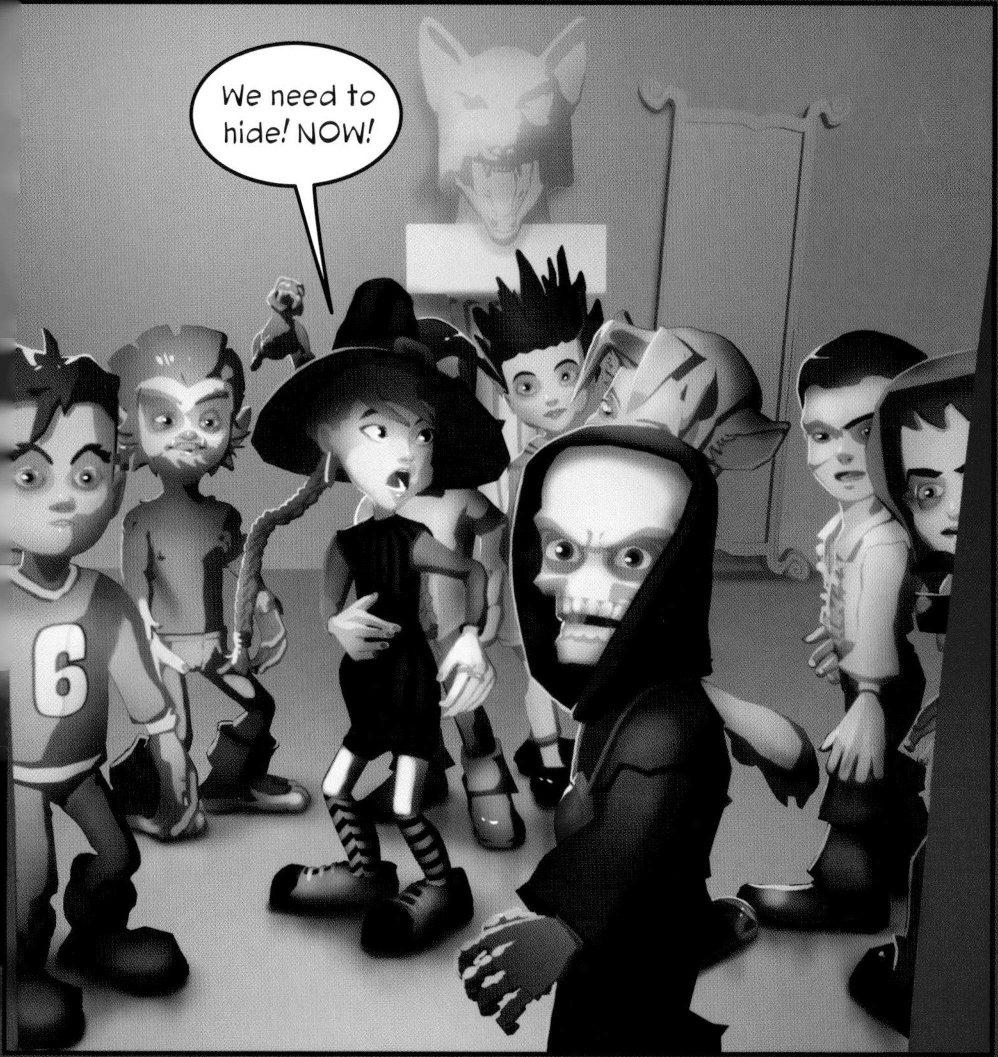
We need to hide! NOW!

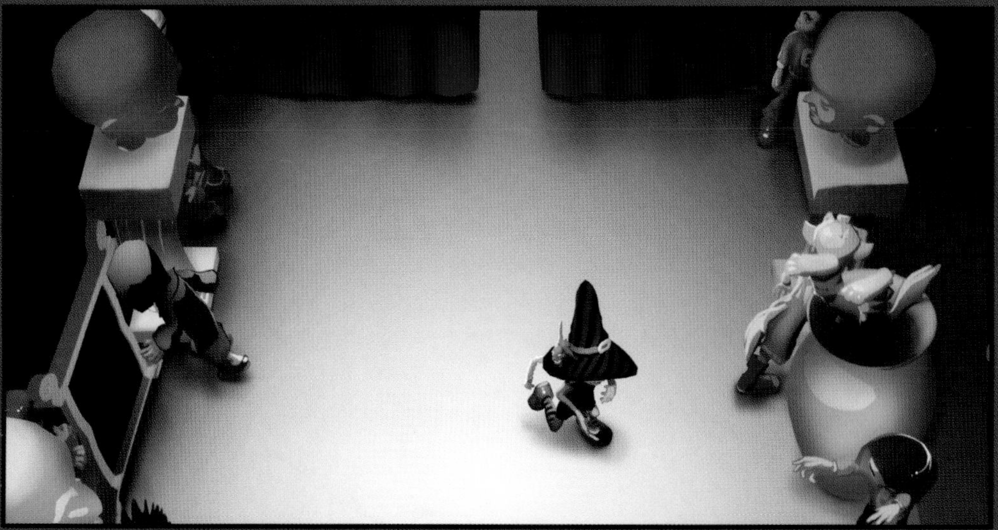

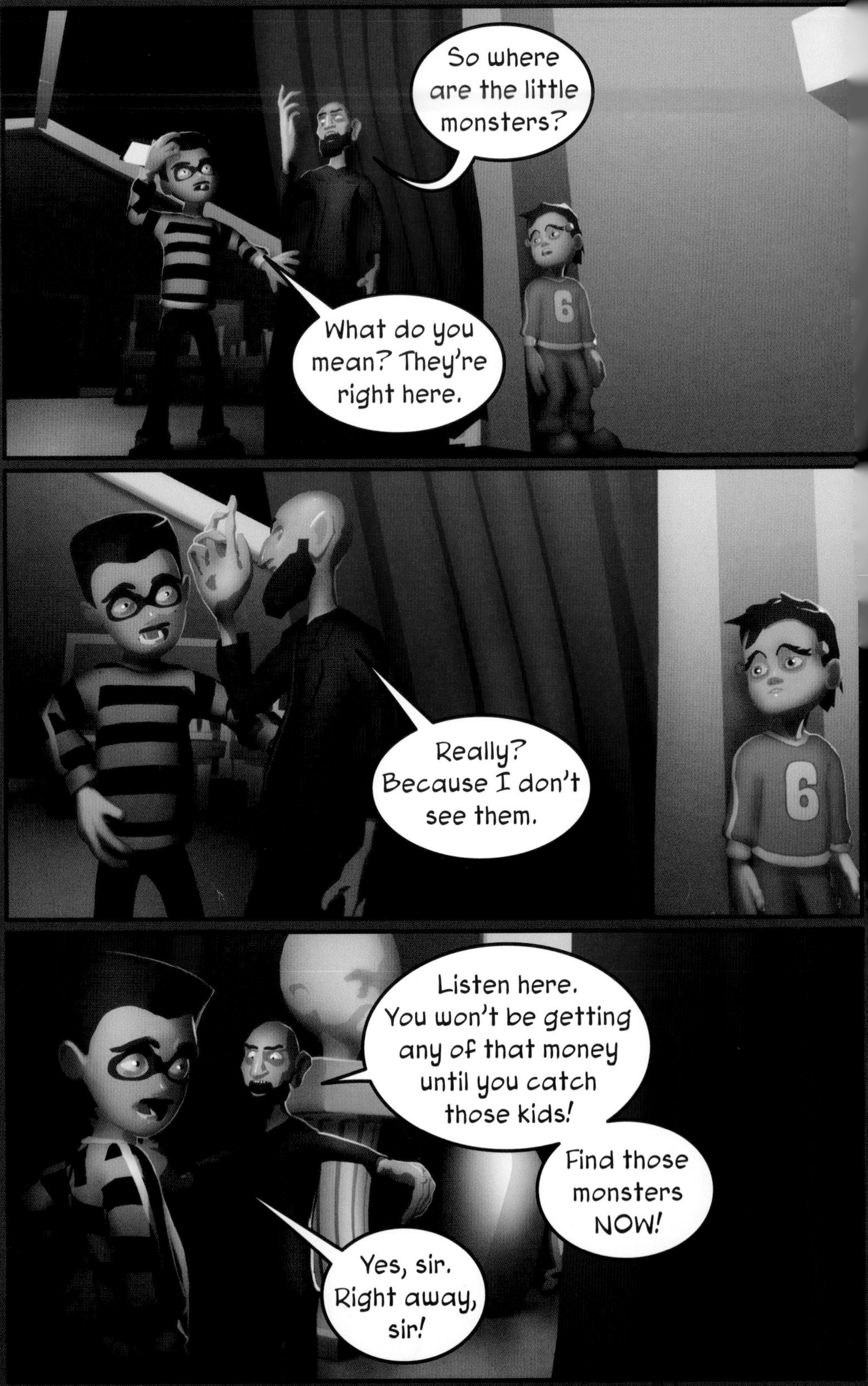
So where are the little monsters?
What do you mean? They're right here.
Really? Because I don't see them.
Listen here. You won't be getting any of that money until you catch those kids!
Find those monsters NOW!
Yes, sir. Right away, sir!

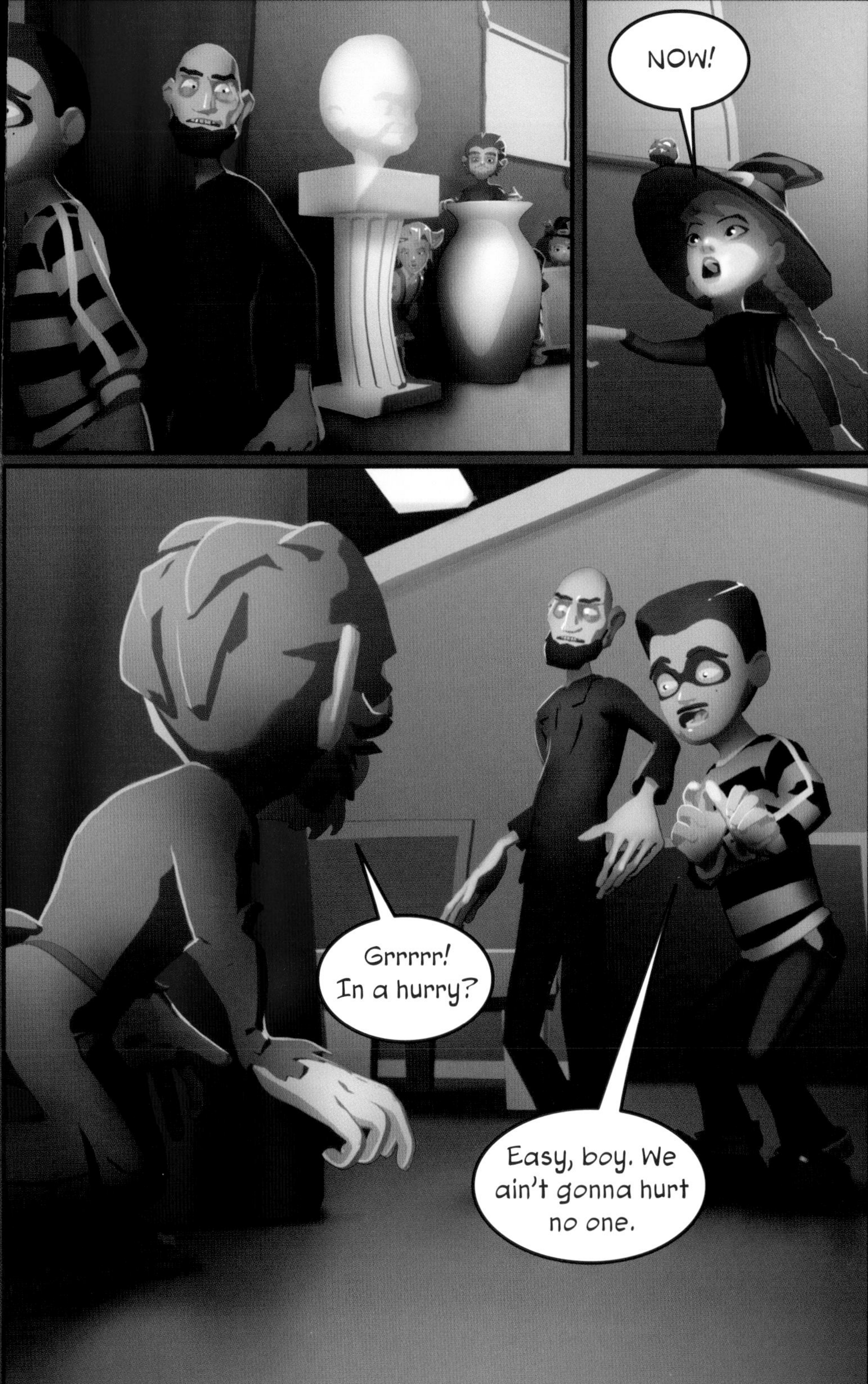
NOW!
Grrrrr!
In a hurry?
Easy, boy. We ain't gonna hurt no one.

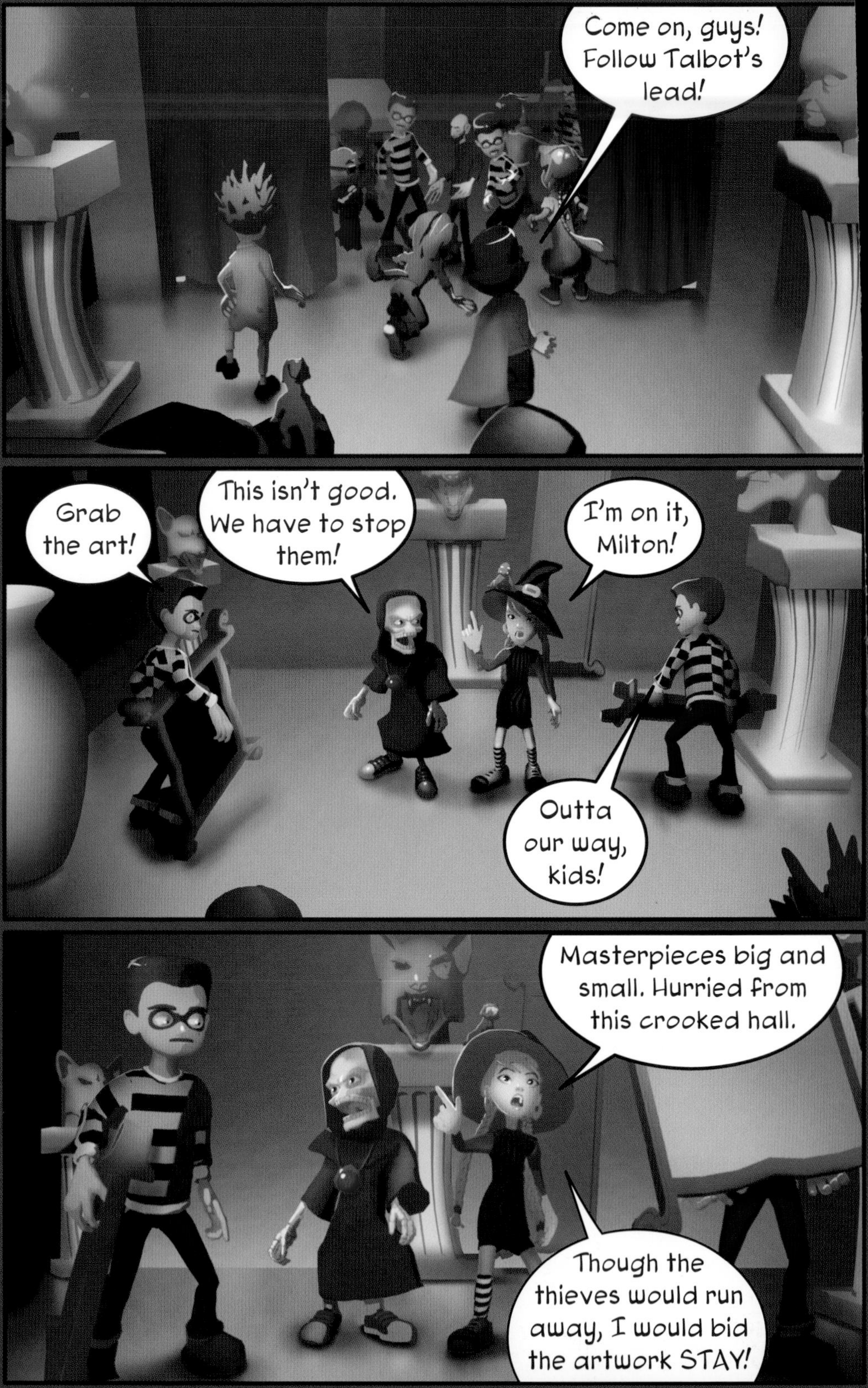
Come on, guys! Follow Talbot's lead!
Grab the art!
This isn't good. We have to stop them!
I'm on it, Milton!
Outta our way, kids!
Masterpieces big and small. Hurried from this crooked hall.
Though the thieves would run away, I would bid the artwork STAY!

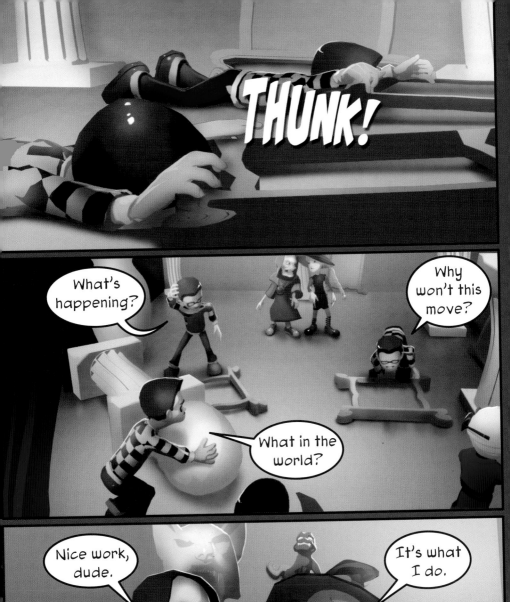

THUNK!

What's happening?

Why won't this move?

What in the world?

Nice work, dude.

It's what I do.

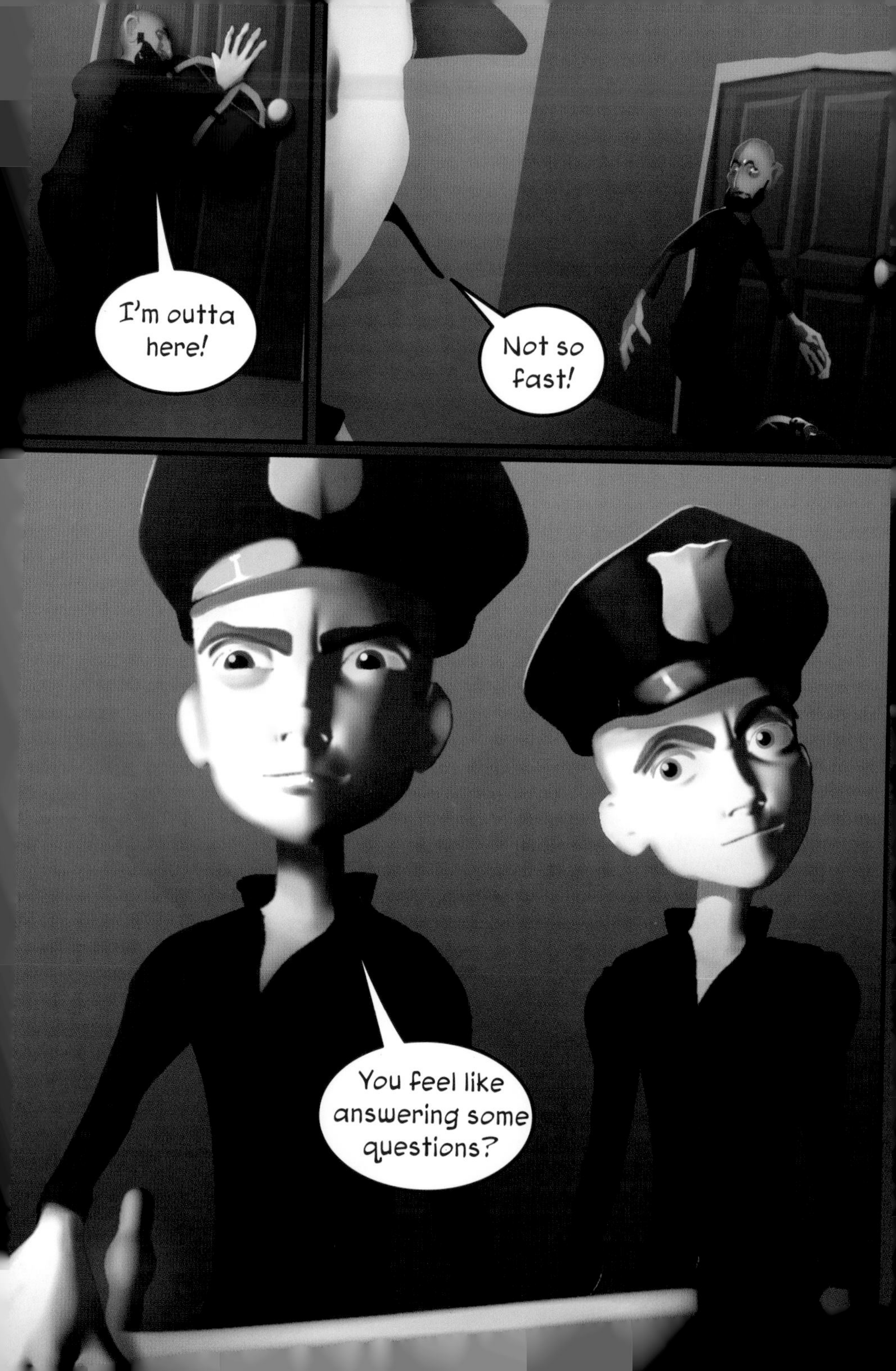

I'm outta here!
Not so fast!
You feel like answering some questions?

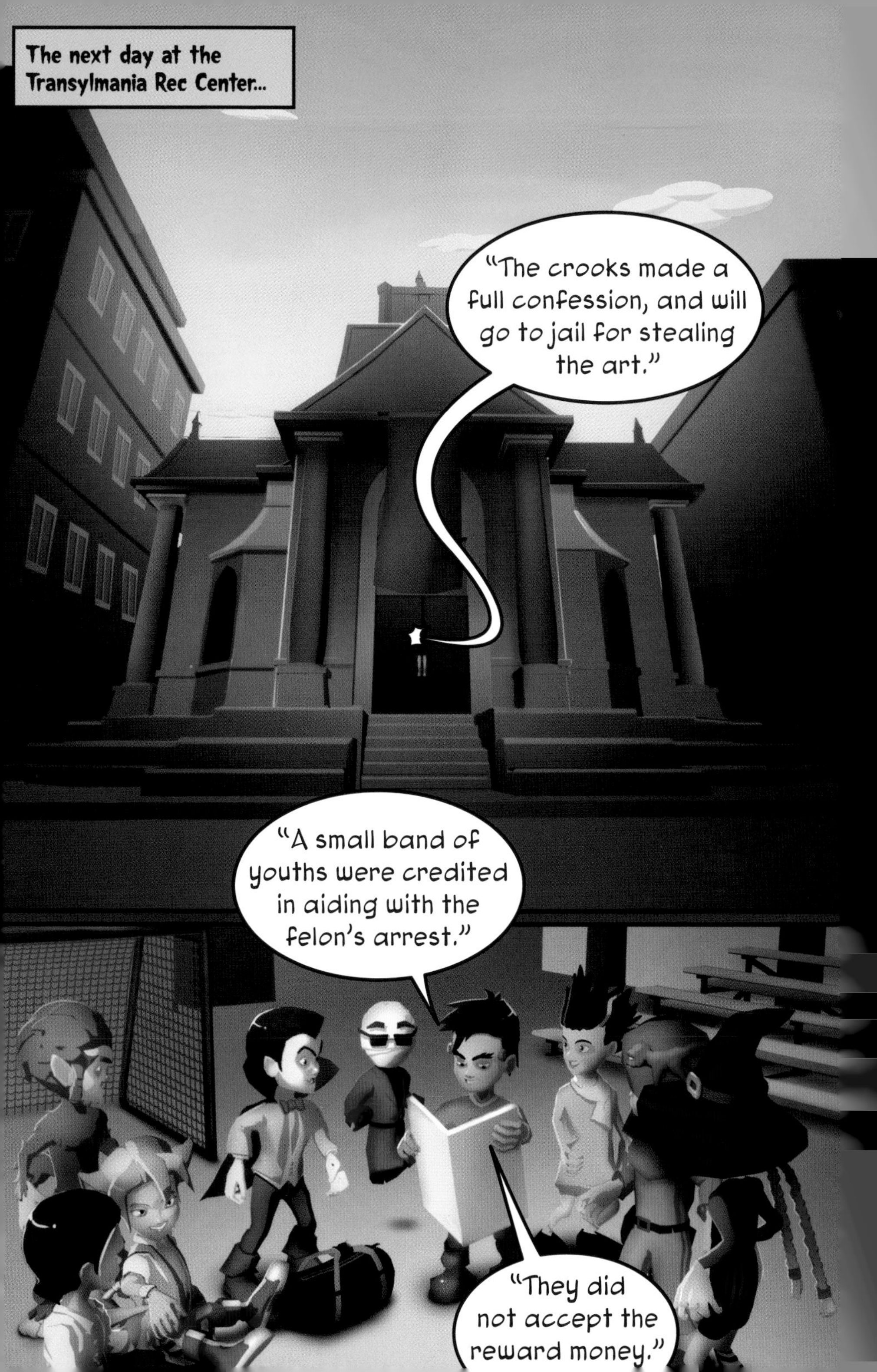
The next day at the Transylmania Rec Center...
"The crooks made a full confession, and will go to jail for stealing the art."
"A small band of youths were credited in aiding with the felon's arrest."
"They did not accept the reward money."

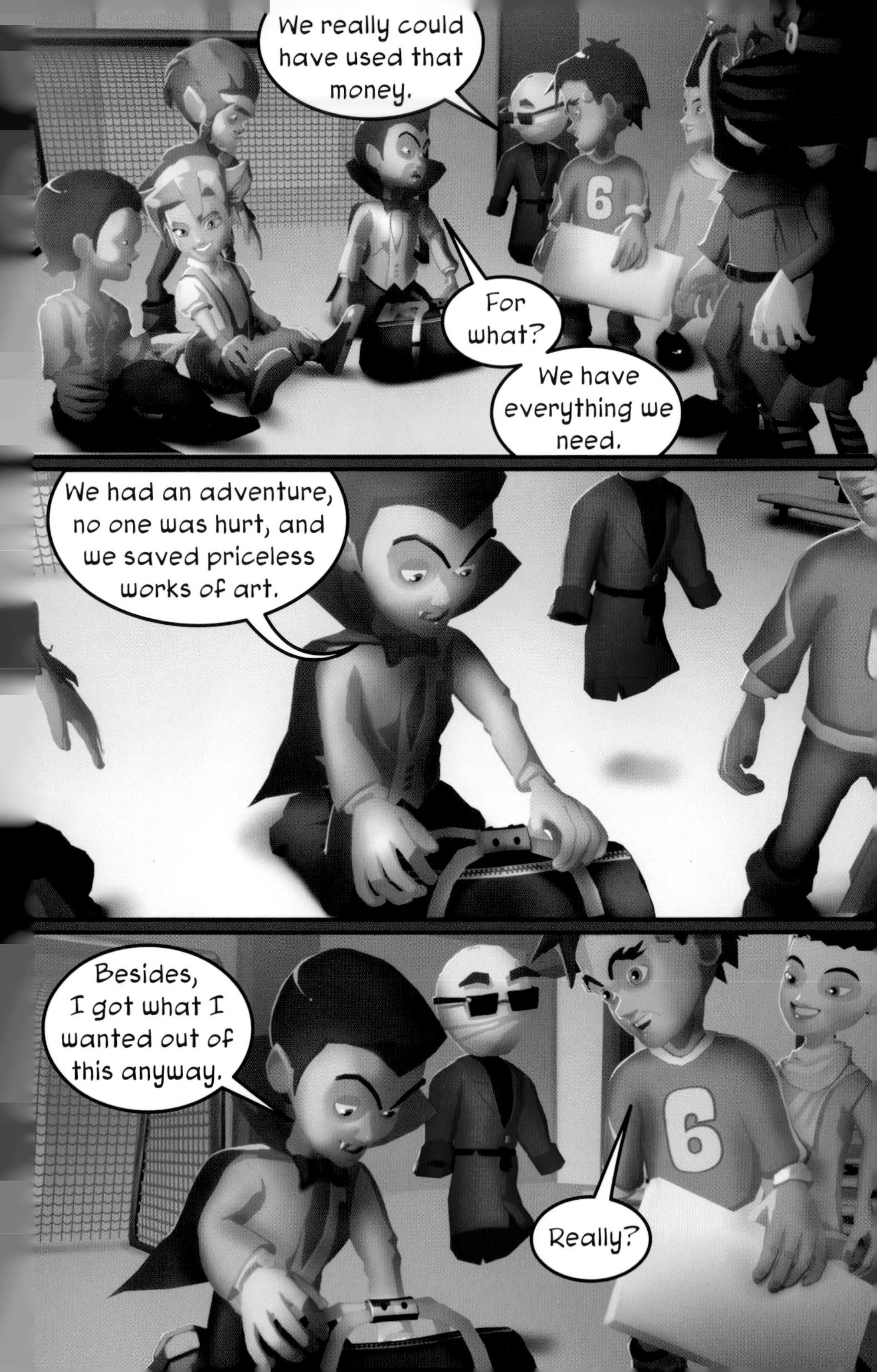
We really could have used that money.
For what?
We have everything we need.
We had an adventure, no one was hurt, and we saved priceless works of art.
Besides, I got what I wanted out of this anyway.
Really?

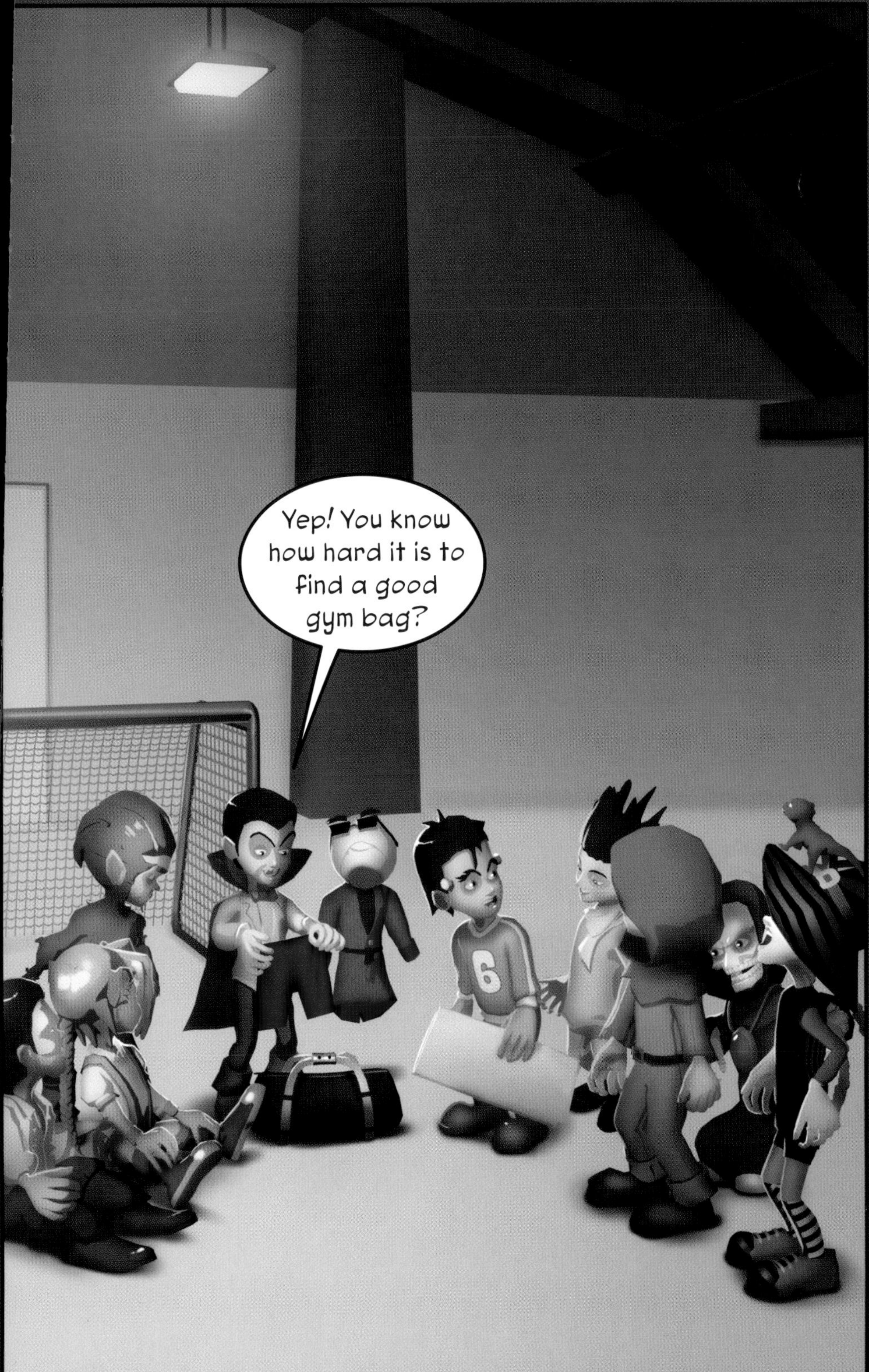
Yep! You know how hard it is to find a good gym bag?

FAMOUS ART HEISTS

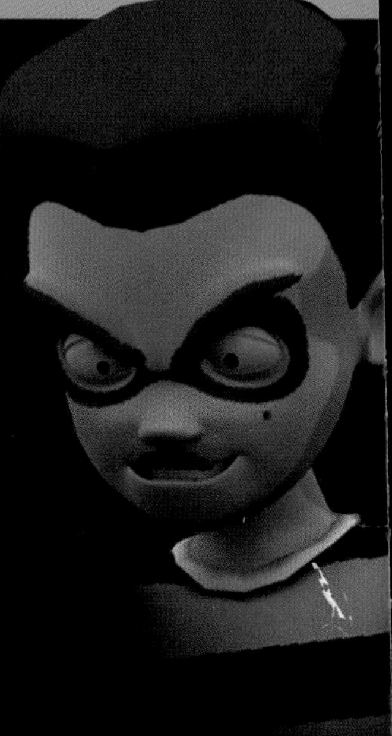

—In 1911, Leonardo da Vinci's famous *Mona Lisa* painting was stolen from the Louvre museum in Paris, France. Vincenzo Peruggia stole the painting while he was working. It was found two years later.

—In 1990, the biggest art heist in U.S. history took place at the Isabella Stewart Gardner Museum in Boston. Two men claiming to be police officers handcuffed security guards and shut off the alarm system. They took thirteen pieces, which included works by Vermeer, Rembrandt, and Manet. All of the items are still missing.

—In 2003, three paintings by Van Gogh, Picasso, and Gauguin were stolen from the Whitworth Gallery in Manchester, England. The thieves avoided cameras, alarms, and guards to take the famous works. A note was left saying that the pieces were stolen to point out how bad the security was at the gallery. All three paintings were found the next day, stuffed behind a toilet at a subway station.

—In 2004, two famous Edvard Munch pieces were stolen from the Munch Museum in Oslo, Norway. Thieves with guns walked into the museum and took *The Scream* and *Madonna*. The paintings were recovered with slight damage in 2006.

GLOSSARY

adventure (ad-VEN-chur)—an exciting experience

confession (kuhn-FESS-shun)—a statement admitting guilt

faint (FAYNT)—not very strong

favor (FAY-vur)—something helpful or kind that you do for someone

felons (FEL-uhnz)—people who have committed a serious crime

masterpieces (MASS-tur-pees-ez)—outstanding pieces of work

scent (SENT)—a smell

thieves (THEEVZ)—people who steal things

DISCUSSION QUESTIONS

1. Vlad was super excited to show his friends his bag. What did you think Vlad had in his gym bag?

2. The monsters decided not to call the police. Do you think they should have? Explain your answer.

3. The monsters didn't take the reward money. Would you have taken the reward? Why or why not?

WRITING PROMPTS

1. Witchita comes up with a great spell to stop the art thieves. Write your own spell to stop the crooks.

2. Write a small article for the local newspaper about the monsters and their heroic efforts in catching the art thieves.

3. Pick your favorite monster and write a small paragraph explaining why you like him or her.

ABOUT
SEAN O'REILLY
AND ARCANA STUDIO

As a lifelong comics fan, Sean O'Reilly dreamed of becoming a comic book creator. In 2004, he realized that dream by creating Arcana Studio. In one short year, O'Reilly took his studio from a one-person operation in his basement to an award-winning comic book publisher with more than 150 graphic novels produced for Harper Collins, Simon & Schuster, Random House, Scholastic, and others.

Within a year, the company won many awards including the Shuster Award for Outstanding Publisher and the Moonbeam Award for top children's graphic novel. O'Reilly also won the Top 40 Under 40 award from the city of Vancouver and authored The Clockwork Girl for Top Graphic Novel at Book Expo America in 2009. Currently, O'Reilly is one of the most prolific independent comic book writers in Canada. While showing no signs of slowing down in comics, he now writes screenplays and adapts his creations for the big screen.

Mighty Mighty MONSTERS ADVENTURES

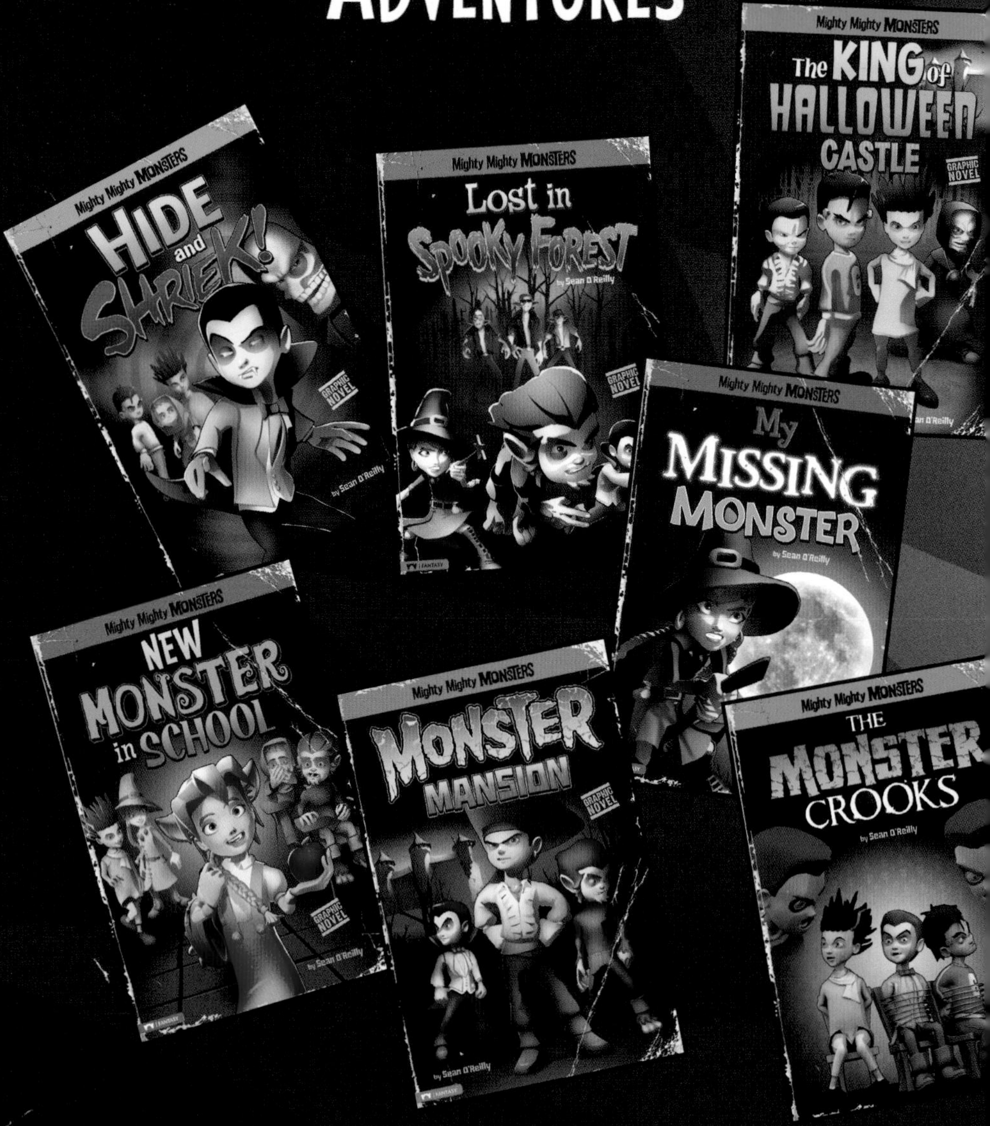
Mighty Mighty MONSTERS
The KING of HALLOWEEN CASTLE
GRAPHIC NOVEL
Mighty Mighty MONSTERS
HIDE and SHRIEK!
GRAPHIC NOVEL
by Sean O'Reilly
Mighty Mighty MONSTERS
Lost in Spooky Forest
by Sean O'Reilly
GRAPHIC NOVEL
Mighty Mighty MONSTERS
My Missing Monster
by Sean O'Reilly
Mighty Mighty MONSTERS
NEW MONSTER in SCHOOL
GRAPHIC NOVEL
by Sean O'Reilly
Mighty Mighty MONSTERS
MONSTER MANSION
GRAPHIC NOVEL
by Sean O'Reilly
Mighty Mighty MONSTERS
THE MONSTER CROOKS
by Sean O'Reilly

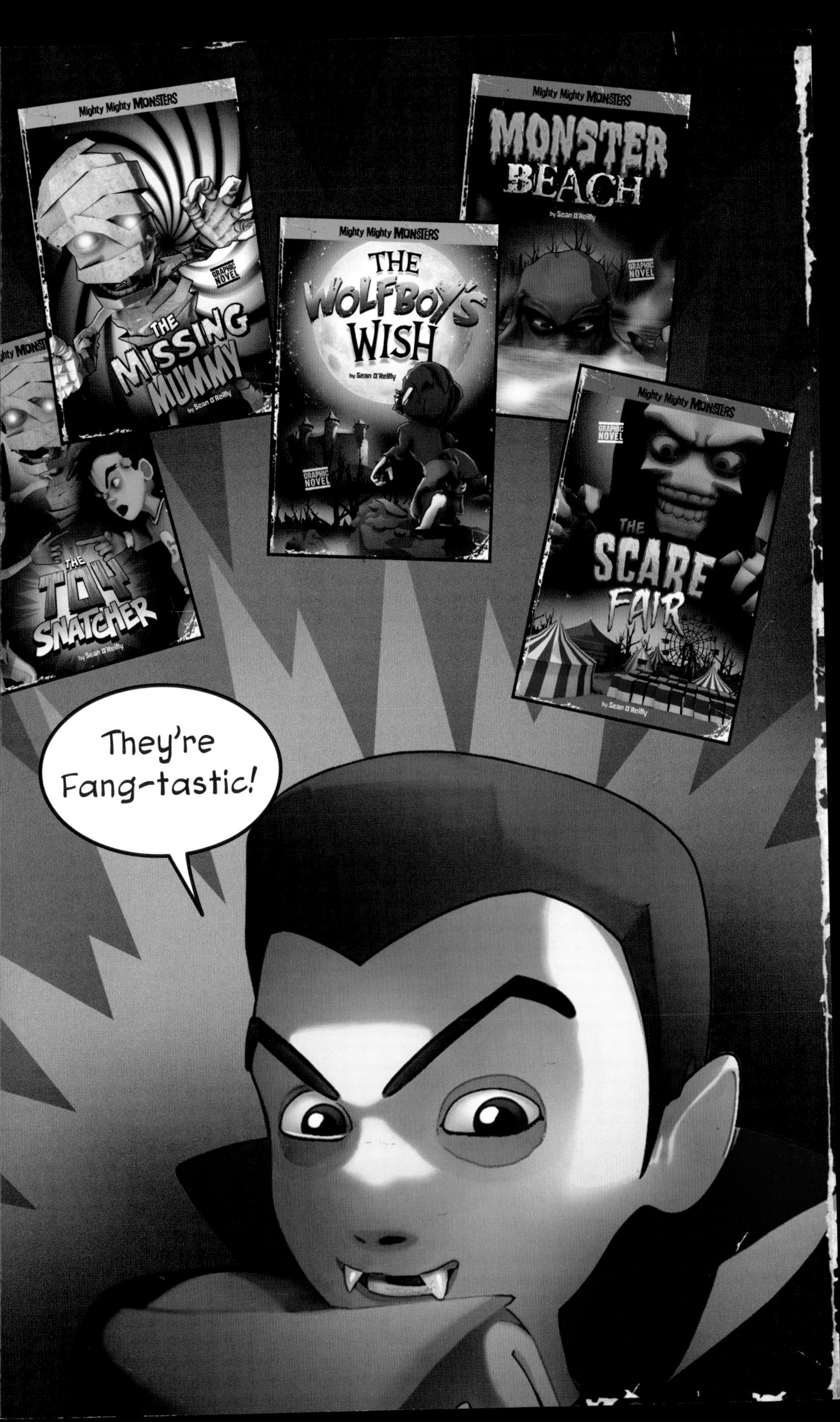
Mighty Mighty MONSTERS
THE MISSING MUMMY
by Sean O'Reilly
GRAPHIC NOVEL
Mighty Mighty MONSTERS
THE WOLFBOY'S WISH
by Sean O'Reilly
GRAPHIC NOVEL
Mighty Mighty MONSTERS
MONSTER BEACH
by Sean O'Reilly
GRAPHIC NOVEL
THE TOY SNATCHER
by Sean O'Reilly
Mighty Mighty MONSTERS
GRAPHIC NOVEL
THE SCARE FAIR
by Sean O'Reilly
They're Fang-tastic!